No Longer Yours

L. L. MOMON

To my family and to my supporters. I love you and thank you for every page you've read. I not only write these stories for me but for you as well. Although this is a complete work of fiction, I'm sure it's someone's truth. If you have or are experiencing domestic violence in any form. Please know it rarely ends well. Leave while you still can. Unfortunately, I've witnessed it enough to know how things can swiftly change but the men often don't. Take the strength you have and run and trust that God will provide. It may actually save your life.

Be Blessed

A book must be the axe for the frozen sea within us.

— FRANZ KAFKA

Prologue

My life changed the minute her name lit up the screen. If I'd known then what I know now, I would have never answered the phone. I would've let that call die in voicemail hell. I would have pressed spam likely, blocked her and blocked my own curiosity. Anything to avoid the chaos and melee that was sure to follow.

I was already in fuck him mode, but hearing the bitch's syrupy voice ooze through the speaker of the phone sent me over the edge. It flipped a switch I didn't even know existed. Something dark woke up in me. Something I couldn't come back from.

My head swooned with thoughts so evil, I scared my damn self. I attempted to pray it away, but that wasn't working either. God's justice moved too slow. Mine needed to happen now. I needed him to hurt, to feel the kind of pain that burrowed under your skin and clawed at your throat until you couldn't breathe.

I laid beside him watching his chest rise and fall for ten minutes, counting every breath, and the entire time I imagined driving a butcher's knife straight through it. I told myself to wait, to play the long game, but patience has a limit, and mine was pushed to the max.

"You're my peace" replayed in my mind like some kind of broken record, one that the needle was stuck on and wouldn't stop no matter how many times I bumped the table. The walls started to feel as if they were closing in on me. Peace, huh. I'm bringing this muthafucka peace when all he's brought me is pain.

CHAPTER 1

Dream On

H ave you ever had a dream so real that it yanked you out of your sleep? One that made you sit straight up in your bed and clung to your skin even after your eyes opened? Lately, those kinds of dreams have been coming too often for my liking.

My mother had a gift. The gift of sight. Some would have called her a seer, but I just called her Mama. She could see things beyond the spiritual realm. Sniffing out sickness before symptoms hit. Knowing who was pregnant before they did and who would be next to walk down the aisle. She also knew who was getting cheated on and whose man wasn't worth a shit. My mother wasn't a creepy type of seer. She didn't need crystals, candles, or to stare into your soul. She wouldn't pull out any cards, consult any spirits, or ask you to hold her hand. She simply just... knew.

Every man, troubled friend, and frenemy my mother warned me about... turned out to be whatever she said they were. I hated it, but she was always right. It wasn't until my mid-teens that I realized she'd passed that gift down to me. Much like her... I didn't want it, but it lived in me too.

I never tried to hone in on it. I just wanted it to go away, but it never did. It only got stronger. So here I was, a reluctant intuitive. My best friend Pamela kept me on speed dial and called me whenever she started dating someone new. All she had to do was show me a picture, and it was like I could see that person clear as day... and in their element. I could also feel their intentions... good or bad.

I'd take a deep staggered breath, and she would say, "Noooo, friend. Not him. I really liked this one." There would be a pause, and we would crack up laughing. She called me her own personal Mrs. Cleo because I just... knew shit.

Oddly enough, when it came to myself... things were always fuzzy. But lately, my dreams were crystal clear. I remembered them from beginning to end, and it made me question if my marriage was as rock solid as I thought it was. Three nights in a row, visions of Jhovan and an unknown woman invaded my dreams. These dreams were freakishly unsettling, and I wanted to get down to the bottom of it. But how could I roll over and accuse this man of cheating when I had no proof?

The pit of my stomach told me everything I'd dreamed has happened, was happening, or was about to happen. That feeling always unraveled me and gnawed at me. Intuition had a way of sitting on your chest until you listened. One thing was for certain: what's done in the dark always comes to light.

Sitting up in my bed, I shook my thoughts away and picked up my phone to check the time. Light the color of warm honey poured from my blinds, signaling the beginning of my day. My babies had to be up soon, so I got up and sauntered to the kitchen to fix a pot of coffee for me and my oldest.

He was only eight years old but loved a good cup of Joe. I'd always said that he was my grandfather reincarnated. Same old soul, same love for black coffee. Along with the coffee, I quickly whipped up a pot of grits, eggs, sausage, and buttered toast.

By the time everything was done, Jhovan Jr. was headed toward me with his arms out, reaching for a hug. Of course, I obliged. My children were three of the sweetest, kindest, well-mannered children in this neighborhood, and for that... I was a proud mama.

They were not morning people, so I had to find ways

to get them going in the A.M. Music always did the trick, so I began most mornings blasting the stereo.

"Alexa, play music by Cleo Sol and turn it up to the highest volume." Music filled the kitchen, smooth, airy, healing. Within minutes, the house came alive.

I heard footsteps trampling down the stairs.

"Good morning, Mama, and good morning, Jr.," Thalia, my seven-year-old, said as she trekked toward me.

"Mama, I want a hug too. Don't forget about me," Trinity, my five-year-old, said as she rubbed the sleep from her eyes before snuggling next to her brother.

Laughing, I gathered them and gave them a big bear hug before escorting them to the bathrooms to get them ready for school. Once we were done, we headed back to the kitchen where I fixed plates, handed Jr. his little iced coffee, and ascended upstairs to get myself ready to sit in the drop-off line.

Even with the music blasting, Jhovan was still sound asleep. Not wanting to wake him, I quietly slipped back into the bedroom, then the bathroom to take a quick shower. A few minutes into my shower, I felt a draft. I looked up and saw my husband standing there, naked as a jaybird and dick standing at attention. My pussy purred as I watched his thickness bounce while he walked toward me. My husband was fine... not fine fine, but the kind of handsome that crept up on you with a sly smile or the raise of a brow.

He stood 6'1, 225 pounds of pure muscle that he worked extra hard to achieve. Abs that looked like a washboard and his arms made me want to melt into them every time I saw them. He was so sexy to me, and that was all that mattered.

"Jhovan, damn baby. That dick sure is dicking this morning," I giggled. I don't have time though. The babies are downstairs eating, and they're ready to go. As soon as I'm done in here, I'm loading them up and getting them off to school. Keep it up for me. I'm gonna sit on it when I get back."

"Why not now, Zaya? It won't take that long. I promise I'll be quick. In and out just like a robbery," he said as he stroked his throbbing manhood.

"That's what you say now, but you've never been a minute man. Am I supposed to believe that you are starting today? Trust me, I want to make love too, but just give me a little time, please. I've got to drop off precious cargo, and I'll be right back."

Sucking his teeth, he muttered. "Yeah, whatever. You need to stop babying them anyway. You can put their asses on the bus like normal people do. I don't see why you need to drive them to school every day. Shit, they get all the attention around here. Your own husband can't even get his dick wet because you always have something to do."

"I beg your pardon. These are my children...our children. You act like I'm doing this shit for someone else's kids. Excuse me for giving a fuck about our offspring. I thought being a loving mother was in. For your information, I drop them off each morning because I enjoy being the last face they see before they walk into the schoolhouse. I love seeing my babies wave goodbye to me and blow me kisses. It's the sweetest thing ever, but I guess you wouldn't know that feeling. Your ass has never dropped them off in the morning, so I could see how you wouldn't understand." I spat as I turned the water off and grabbed my towel.

"I don't have time for this shit this morning, Zaya. I'm gonna hit up the gym and get a workout in before heading into the office. I've got to get some kind of stimulation from somewhere. I sure as hell ain't getting it here," he quipped as he started the water back up and stepped into the shower.

Ignoring him, I dried off, quickly lotioned my body, got dressed, and ran back down the stairs. Loading everyone into my SUV, I drove them to school. As I sat patiently in the drop-off line, my phone rang. I thought it was Jhovan calling to apologize, but I was wrong. It was my best friend, Pamela.

"Good morning, bestie," I chirped.

"Good morning, Chica. Let me guess...you're in the drop-off line?"

"I am, and you are on speakerphone, so please don't say anything crazy," I quickly muttered before she got started. Pamela had a filthy mouth, and the last thing I needed was my children heading into this school where I paid a hefty tuition, cursing and acting like they didn't have any home training.

"Girl, shut up. I don't need any disclaimers. I know that my babies can hear me. Heyyyyy, my sugars," she screamed through the Bluetooth.

"Good morning, Titi Pamela," they all said in unison.

She giggled and said, "Call me back when you get them situated. I've got something to tell you."

"Ok, friend...will do," I said before disconnecting the call.

Still sitting, I rolled my window down to enjoy the fresh morning air. It was fall yet still warm, but you could catch a nice breeze before eight a.m. Seconds after my window was down, a tall, freckled-faced woman waved, and Jr. waved back.

"Ummm, do you know her, baby? Who is that?"

"That's the teacher's assistant. Her name is Ms. Fortress. She's really nice. She lets us stay out on the playground a little longer than we are supposed to...if we've been good," he said cheerfully.

"Well, that sure is nice of her. I thought I knew all the teachers. Did she just start?"

"Yes, Mama. The other teacher went out on mallernity leave," he said so innocently.

Giggling, "You mean maternity leave, baby."

"Yes, Mama. That's what I said."

"My bad. I guess I misheard you. It's time to unbuckle your seatbelts. Here comes Mrs. Lynn."

All three filed out of the SUV like little soldiers, yelling, "I love you, Mama," before they grabbed each other's hand and walked into the building. I waved goodbye while catching my kisses and pulled off. I phoned Jhovan to see if he was still at home, but he didn't answer. I guess he was still in his feelings. So I called Pamela back to see what she wanted.

She answered with, "Are those babies out of that car? Cause girl...they damn sure couldn't hear this shit I had to tell you. Bitch, I'm mad enough to bite the bark off a tree." I could hear the scowl in her voice.

"Yes, they are in school. What has happened now?" I asked.

"Well, I just got a call from my doctor's office. It was my yearly, and I had them run a full STD panel."

"Ok and..."

"And the nurse just called to tell me that I had Trichomonas."

"Ok, Pamela, enlighten me. What in the hell is a Trichomonas?" I asked as I pulled into my subdivision.

"Apparently, it's a sexually transmitted disease caused by a dick parasite. It's something you get from hunching on nasty peen," she said casually.

I screamed laughing. "Are you fucking kidding me? You mean to tell me that Ross gave you a disease?"

"He sure the fuck did, and I'm fucking his world up as soon as I see him. I tried calling him this morning to see if we could meet up, but I'm guessing that the jobless bastard is still asleep. It's not like he has somewhere to be." She smacked her lips.

"Pamela...you know I don't wanna be that bitch to say I told you so, but I did. I told you he had ulterior motives. He wasn't after your heart. He was after your money and what you could offer his broke ass. You were always too good for him. Don't get me wrong, he was nice, but he was a hobosexual. No job, no education, no apartment or house, and he still lives with his mama. Like...nothing to offer you. The only thing Ross added to your life was a nice face and a big dick."

"I know, I know, Zaya. But that thang was just so good. I'm talking about innnnn itttt. I guess now I know why. He had little parasite dick helpers."

I hollered laughing. "Please shut up, Pamela. You are so damn stupid. Promise me something...the next time you meet a man hanging out at a gas station, you'll leave him there."

"But who else is going to wash my windows and pump my gas for a dollar?" she cackled.

"I know that you are only making jokes because you secretly want to crash out. I know you've got to be hurt. I would be. Because even though he turned out not to be shit, he was fine as fuck and charming. I also know you really liked him, and I'm sorry that it went down the way it did."

"You ain't never lied, bestie. I have to laugh to keep from crying. How could I be so damn stupid? I should have been making these kinds of fuck-ups when I was younger. I'm almost forty years old."

"Don't be so hard on yourself, girl. We have all been stupid for someone. It just took you a lot longer than most to find someone to be stupid over," I giggled.

"I know, Zaya, but I can't believe that at my big grown age...I let this happen. I'm kicking my own ass. I knew better than to have been fucking on someone without first seeing his Mychart. Now that I think about it, he probably doesn't have one." She drew in a long breath. "Now, for the next seven days I can't even have a drink to calm my nerves because I'm on antibiotics. I can't smoke either because my job is quick to throw a drug test on us. I guess I'm just going to have to raw dog life."

"Pamela, I hope this is your lesson learned because it could always have been worse. Be thankful that it was only a parasite. It could have been those three alphabets. Anyway, boo, Jhovan went to the gym this morning, then will head to work. I'm going to be alone until it's time to go get the kids. I could make us some snacks, and we can watch a movie if you want."

"You are so right, and I am thankful, but I'm still pissed. Listen, I would love to come over to your cozy place and bask in the glow of being a housewife for a while, but I can't. I have work in a few. A twelve-hour shift, so I've got to get ready. As you know...crime never sleeps."

"I know, Mrs. Officer. Weeee oh weeee oh weee, weee oh weee-," I whispered.

"Shut uuup," she screamed. "I knew your dumb ass was going to do that. Why do you have to sing that song every damn time?" she said, laughing into the phone.

"Because it's so catchy. Anyway, have a beautiful day at work, go fight crime, take care of yourself, don't hurt nobody, and don't let nobody hurt you. Call me when you get off, ok, bestie? I love you."

CHAPTER 2

Box of Goodies

I hung up the phone and sauntered into the house. Jhovan had taken his shower and left his clothes where he stepped out of them. I saw them lying there and kept walking. I wasn't his maid. I already picked up after three people in this house. I didn't need a fourth.

Since he was off getting exercise, I followed suit. I changed into a Lulu Lemon outfit and trekked off for a run in my neighborhood. It was still early and nice outside. After running three miles, I came back home to see Jhovan's car in the driveway. I walked into the house to find a bouquet of roses waiting for me.

I sat there staring at them for a while when he came out of nowhere.

"Hey babe, is that you?" I heard him say as I walked through the kitchen.

"Who else would it be, Jhovan? Of course it's me. These flowers are beautiful. Are they mine?"

"Yes, they're for you," he whispered as he stood behind me, wrapping his arms around my waist. "I realized I kind of overreacted this morning. I'm sorry for getting upset with you. Especially about something so trivial. Things haven't been great at work, and I've been a little frustrated lately. That's no excuse though because I shouldn't have taken that tone with you."

He leaned down and kissed me on my neck, which was my spot. He flipped me around and licked my lips while unzipping my top. Stopping his hand, I grabbed the handle and zipped it back up.

"Jhovan...stooooop," I whined. "I just ran three miles and I'm all sweaty. At least let me go wash some of this funk off before you try to seduce me."

I walked away. Grabbing me by the hand, he pulled me towards him. Leaning in, he stared into my eyes and whispered, "Girl, please. That's just how I want it. I like my pussy with a little twang to it. I don't want you washing off all that goodness. How about you let me lick it off."

He caught me off guard, so I blinked at him, trying to gauge if he was serious. He was. We'd done some nasty shit before, but licking three-mile pussy was new to me.

He grabbed my zipper handle, slid it down, and licked the sweat from between my double D breasts. A shiver ran down my spine, and my pussy started to grow slick. Grabbing me by the waist, he picked me up and gently sat me on the countertop. Tugging at my pants, I raised my lower region so he could slide them down.

He threw them to the floor, grabbed my knees, opened my legs, revealing my aching, throbbing clit.

"I've been thinking about doing this since I saw you in the shower this morning," he whispered in my ear. "I want to lick every drop from you."

He softly kissed my thighs, teasing and taunting before sliding his tongue across the crease of my pussy and taking my clit into his mouth. He sucked it ever so gently before stopping and sliding his tongue down to my ass.

"Zaya, gawwwt damn girl. Even your ass sweat taste good," he said before tongue fucking my asshole. He spit in it before sliding his pinkie in as his mouth found my clit again. He began attacking it with his tongue. Licking, sucking, and slurping. He then slid a finger in my center while he talked that shit that drove me crazy.

"Yeah, Zaya...Give me all that nut. I want you to cum for me, baby." He slurped again, sucking like he owed me money. My clit was throbbing so hard and standing at full attention. It was clear what was coming next.

He started to finger fuck me harder while his finger remained in my ass. "I want you to squirt for daddy. Give it to me, Zaya. Give it to me. Don't hold back...Push that shit out. Buss that muthafuckin nut."

My body was overwhelmed with pleasure. My pussy started doing involuntary Kegels, contracting and quaking while I tried to steady my breathing. I tried to hold back, but he wasn't letting up.

"Jhovan, baby. Please...Please...it's too much," I moaned. "It's too tender."

"I...Don't...Give...A...Fuck, Zaya. Fuck my face and buss that muthafuckin nut in my mouth. Bear down and give it to me. Do it now, Zaya...give me what I want," he demanded.

I loved when he talked dirty to me. I did what I was told. He was pumping like he was waiting for oil to surface and finally...my pussy turned into a geyser. I squirted pussy nectar all in his mouth and he caught it all. He guzzled it like it was Gatorade, not wasting a drop.

"Oooh yes, baby. That's what I needed. I want all that natural moisturizer. You taste so muthafuckin' good." Sliding down his pants, he pulled me closer to the edge and slid right into my center. There was no resistance. His body was still wet with my essence.

He fucked me so hard that silverware and a glass dropped to the floor. He didn't stop. Nor did he slow down to savor the moment. There was no mercy. I thought he would put me through the damn granite. Over and over, he slid in and out of my pussy like a madman and I loved it.

"Jhovan, damn baby. You wanted this pussy bad, didn't you?" I moaned through the pumps.

"I love to feel your walls curve to my dick. You feel so good, Zaya. So warm." He grunted.

I tried to fuck back but he was fucking me so hard...there was no use. Jhovan was a big dude, the force behind each thrust shut me down. He and I were both so engulfed with pleasure, neither of us heard the doorbell ring. I was biting and scratching, and he was sucking and moaning. Both completely insatiable. By the time we climaxed, we were exhausted.

I peeled myself from the granite as he tipped out of the kitchen.

"Just stay right there, baby. I got a little carried away." He chuckled as he tiptoed around the broken glass to retrieve my shoes.

"Oh, don't worry. I am. You are not about to have me around here cut up. You had my legs spread so wide... I believe you dislocated my hip." I chuckled.

"Are you alright over there? Girl, you had me cutting up. Your pussy juice is some kind of potion. That shit had me out my mind. I know you like to take control, but I decided to switch it up a little bit. Let you know that you aren't the only one around here that can dominate.

Ummm... I... I hope I didn't go too far with the pinkie in the ass. I know we don't do ass play, but I figured a little pinkie couldn't hurt." He grabbed the broom from the pantry and began cleaning up the mess.

I slid on my shoes, hopped down, and grabbed the silverware from the floor. "I'm perfectly fine. I didn't mind, it just caught me by surprise. Now don't do that shit again though because I don't like my ass to be tampered with. That's an exit, not an entrance."

"You didn't seem to mind when I tongue fucked you... what does a little pinkie hurt?"

"Shidd, it hurts me. Your hands aren't exactly small, you know. Anyway, Jhovan, now that you are back from the gym, I was thinking we could go outside and start putting up that Gazebo we bought. It's starting to feel good at night and I want to be able to sit out back and relax. Oh, and let's go by Lowes while we are at it. They have this firepit I want. It's only $300 and it's easy to assemble. I'll put it together while you work on the Gazebo."

"Hold on now, Zaya. I'm not home for good. I have work today. I called the guys and told them I would be there, but I would be late."

"Jhovan. You are the damn boss. You can go in when you get ready. There are things that need to be done around this house. You told me months ago we would get started. I mean, there is no time like the present."

"I know, baby, but there is only one me. Unfortunately, I don't get paid to put things up in the backyard. I have a few estimates to take care of, not to mention we have a bid to run in the morning. I'm sorry, Zaya, but that shit is going to have to wait until another day."

Sucking my teeth, I muttered, "That's what you always say. You can find time for everything but the things I need you to do. Would you rather I call someone else and have them put it together? I can contact someone from that handyman website."

"Hell no, you will not. I'm a damn general contractor. What would I look like having another man come to my house to handle something I could easily take care of myself?"

"That's my point. You can take care of it, but you don't have the time, baby. You just said it yourself."

"I tell you what...let me get through this week and I'll get to it this weekend. I promise." He kissed my lips. "Thank you for being such a loving and understanding wife. I know dealing with me and my crazy schedule isn't easy, but you make it work. Just know, you are the sole reason our household runs so smoothly. You the shit, baby."

"Thank you, Jhovan. Thank you for recognizing the

effort I put in. I appreciate that. Oh, I meant to tell you that I spoke with my old boss, India. She has a position open and told me she'd consider me if I were truly ready to come back."

"Why do you want to go back to work, Zaya? I take care of everything. I don't need you to do anything but what you're doing," he said as he grabbed the dustpan and swept up the glass.

"Jhovan, I'm not about to do this with you. This isn't about you. It's about me. The agreement was I would go back to work when our last baby turned five. She's five now and in school. You do realize that I had a career when we met, so I don't know why you assumed I would be okay with staying at home forever. I have goals, and I'm going to meet them. I've sat down for nine years. I won't sit down nine more."

He smacked his lips, "We will talk about it later. I've got to get going, Zaya. I'm about to hop in the shower and wash all your goodness off me." He winked.

"I don't know what I'm going to do with your nasty ass. Now I've got to bleach these countertops and mop this floor." I kissed him before he trekked upstairs to get ready for work.

Realizing I'd left my bumbag in the car, I headed to the driveway to get it. I opened a door and found a beautifully wrapped box sitting on the porch with my name on it. I went to the SUV, and on my way back in, I grabbed the box and went back in the house.

Sitting on the couch, I began to unwrap the package. On the top of the tissue paper was a letter with a heavy floral scent. It was as if someone sprayed it with cheap perfume. Once I got past the putrid smell, I began to read.

> Zaya,
> I hope this package ends up on the right doorstep. Your husband left these at my house. I don't have a need for any of it, so it's yours for the taking. Oh, I wanted him to have these. He loves to smell the scent of my pussy after I've worn them all day. Enclosed is a pair of my panties for him to cherish. I took these off after a twelve-hour shift. He should love them. Enjoy. Muah 💋

I quickly dug down into the box to find its contents: a pair of boxers, a magnum condom wrapper, and a pair of worn panties.

I was disgusted, shocked, but most of all, I was heartbroken.

I sat frozen in the same spot in a daze. Anger coursed through my veins. Heat covered my head like a helmet, but

I couldn't move. My eyes stayed locked on that box like it was alive, daring me to look again.

Upstairs, I could hear the shower running. Jhovan was singing some old R&B song like his world was perfect... like mine hadn't just shattered into a thousand damn pieces.

My hands shook as I lifted the panties from the box again using a pen. They were pink with lace...cheap and cheesy. Some shit I would never wear. They smelled like that floral perfume from the letter, and old pussy. The scent and the thought made me sick to my stomach.

"Twelve-hour shift," I whispered, repeating the words from the letter. "He should love them."

I laughed...not a happy laugh. The kind that held back tears and rage at the same time.

That man had the nerve to kiss me this morning, fuck me like a slut, then tell me I was the reason the household ran so smoothly. "You the shit, Zaya." And all along, he was out here leaving his damn boxers at another bitch's house. This can't be real life. The longer I sat there and thought about it, the angrier I became.

My chest tightened until I thought I might pass out. Suddenly, I heard something drop to the carpet. I looked down and saw blood dripping from my nose. Standing up slowly, I ran to the kitchen to grab a paper towel, still gripping the letter in one hand and the box in the other. There was no way I was touching those shits with my bare hands.

I walked upstairs, quiet at first, then faster. The shower was still running. Steam drifted down the hallway, mixing with the smell of his body wash.

The bathroom door was cracked just enough for me to see his clothes on the counter, his phone lighting up beside the sink.

"Jhovan!" I called out, trying to keep my voice even.

"Yeah, baby?" he answered from behind the glass.

"You forget something?"

CHAPTER 3

Don't Let Her Win

The water stopped. For a second, there was silence.

"What you mean?" he asked.

"Please tell me when you started liking funky pussy... Better yet, funky pussy, ass and panties?" I held up the box, tilting it so he could see the contents. "Does any of these things look familiar to you?"

He froze, his eyes darting from me to the box in my hand.

"Zaya, what is that?"

"You tell me." My voice cracked, but I didn't care. "It was on our porch. Some woman said *you* left these at her house. Said you'd like the smell of her pussy after a twelve-hour shift."

He took a slow step out of the shower, dripping wet, his mouth opening but no words coming out.

"You gonna stand your ass there and act like you don't know what I'm talking about?" I hissed. "Don't even try it, Jhovan. Don't you dare fucking lie."

"Zaya, baby, that's not--"

"Don't 'baby' me! Do I look stupid to you, muthafucka?"

He tried to reach for me, but I stepped back, shaking my head. Tears blurred my vision, but I refused to let them fall.

"All this time," I said quietly, my voice trembling, "I've been holding you down, believing in you, defending you. And this is what I get? Cheap, stinking ass panties and lies?"

He sighed, running a hand over his face. "Zaya, I don't know who would do that, but it ain't what you think."

"Oh, it's *exactly* what I think." I dropped the box onto the wet tile, the contents spilling across the floor. "And you better choose your next words wisely , Jhovan. Because as of right now, I could murder your ass."

Jhovan stared at me like he'd just seen a ghost. His lips parted, but nothing came out at first. Then, finally, his voice cracked through the steam.

"Zaya, listen to me. I can explain."

"Explain what, Jhovan?!" I screamed, stepping closer.

"That you've been fucking around with some trifling bitch? That you've been lying to me, smiling in my face, while she's mailing her dirty panties to my front damn door?"

He flinched at my words, running both hands over his wet head. "It wasn't supposed to be like that."

I laughed bitterly. "Oh, I'm sure it wasn't."

He took a careful step forward, his tone softer now, almost pleading. "It was one time. Just one. I swear to God, Zaya. I fucked up. I was drinking after work, she was there, and it just happened. I felt like shit the second it was over. I ended it before it even started."

I folded my arms across my chest, staring straight through him. "So that makes it better? You think 'one time' is supposed to erase the fact that you disrespected our marriage? Lied to my face? Came home to *me* after being with *her*? Besides, I don't believe that it was just one time. This bitch knows where we live. You've probably been fucking her for a while. It seems like she's known about your stink kink long before I did. And don't lie you bastard. You just licked the sweat off my ass crack."

His eyes filled with panic. "Zaya, please. It meant nothing. I swear on my life, on everything I love, it meant nothing. You're my world, baby. I know I broke your trust, but I can fix this. Please, just... just don't walk away from me."

"You should've thought about that before you stuck your dick in someone else," I snapped.

He stepped closer again, his voice trembling. "You're right. You're right, I fucked up, Zaya... and I'll spend the rest of my life proving to you that I'll never do it again. I'll block her, change my number, curse her out, shiddd...kill her if that's what you want. Whatever it takes. Just don't give up on us. Don't let her win."

That last part made my stomach twist. *"Don't let her win."* Like this was some kind of fucking contest. I shook my head slowly, my voice low and calm now... dangerously calm. "Just what the fuck is she winning? You really don't get it. This isn't about her winning. It's about you losing... me."

He reached for my hand, but I pulled away. His fingertips grazed mine and my skin crawled at the thought of him touching me.

"I love you, Zaya. Please," he whispered.

I looked at him, this man I'd built a life with, standing there, naked and desperate, dripping with water that couldn't wash away what he'd done.

"I don't know if love is enough anymore," I said quietly. Then I turned and walked out of the bathroom, leaving him standing there in the silence he created.

I ran back downstairs, grabbed my purse and keys, and raced toward the front door. Jhovan was on my heels, still dripping, still naked, still begging. I opened the front door; he reached over my head and closed it back.

"Please, please, please don't leave me, Zaya. We can fix this, I promise," he pleaded.

"Get the fuck away from the door before I fuck you up, Jhovan," I scowled.

"Wait, Zaya. At least calm down, please. Your nose is bleeding. That means your blood pressure is up. What happens if you leave and pass out or something like that? What happens then, huh? I promise to leave you alone. I won't say a word. Please, baby, just calm down."

"Fuck you, Jhovan. Like you give a fuck about my well being," I said before pushing him to the side and going out the front door. Please don't come after me either."

Hopping in my SUV, I peeled out of the driveway and started up the road. The only person I could think of was my mother. I placed a call to her.

"Hello, Mama. Are you busy?" I quietly wept.

"Not at all, baby... what's wrong?"

"It's Jhovan. He's having an affair. Some woman mailed her nasty underwear to my house. He said it was just one time, but he was lying. I feel it... I know it, Mama. I've been dreaming about it."

"I know, baby. I've been dreaming about it too. I wanted to call you last week and tell you, but I didn't know what to say or how to say it. I prayed that God gave you the visions that he gave me. My God came through I see."

"He sure did. For three nights straight, I've been having the same dream. Jhovan all hugged up with some woman, but I didn't know who she was. I knew it, Mama. I knew it."

"Listen baby, I just put on a fresh pot of tea. Why don't you stop by and we can talk. It's only an hour drive. It's still early. I promise to let you go in time for you to get my grandbabies from school. Just come on over. We need to talk."

"Ok, Mama... See you in an hour or so."

Steadily crying, I wiped my tears as Jhovan's face appeared on my phone. I swiped left. He called again. I swiped again then placed a call to Pamela but quickly hung up. My bestie was on duty. The last thing I wanted was her distracted because I was having a meltdown about my no-good ass husband. My husband... I was still in disbelief. How could he do this to me?

Trying to calm down, I thought about the softness in my mother's voice. The love and care she'd always given me. Even when my father left and she was hurting, she never let it show. Never turning mean or bitter. She remained kind, humble and present. My children were the light of her life, and she would frequently take the hour drive just to "lay eyes on us," as she would say. She loved us fiercely and looked at Jhovan like a son. I knew she would be disappointed as well.

Men never understand how their actions not only affect the person they're with, but everyone else that's intertwined. It had a terrible snowball effect, and men were none the wiser. My heart was so heavy, as well as my mind. I blindly weaved in and out of traffic while trying to make sense of my life, but the same question plagued me. Why would he do this to me... to us? I thought as I reached 90 on the highway. I was so distraught, I didn't see the state trooper come behind me. My eyes were straight and centered... so much so, he drove up beside me to tell me to pull over.

Slowly, I merged into the emergency lane and put my car in park. I struggled to keep the tears at bay. He slid out of his car and tapped my trunk before walking up to the window.

"Ma'am, can you please roll your window all the way down?"

"Yes, officer," I said as I did what he asked.

"First, are you ok ma'am? Are you in need of medical attention?"

"No officer. Why would you ask that?" I'd completely forgotten about the blood on my shirt.

"Oh, no, officer. I suffer from nosebleeds from time to time. That's it. I'll be fine," I tried to say cheerfully.

"Ok, well I need your license, registration and proof of insurance. Do you know that I clocked you at 87 mph? Do you know that the speed limit on this highway is 65? Where are you going in such a hurry?" he asked as he gazed at the tears rolling down my cheek.

Ignoring his questions, I asked, "May I reach for those things please, sir? I don't want to make any sudden moves and get shot for reaching for something that you told me to reach for."

He chuckled slightly before saying, "Yes, ma'am. Please do and nobody is going to shoot you, ma'am."

"That's what you all say... then bam... I'm dead beside the road and you are hollering put your hands in the air... after you shot me." Without even looking up at him, I placed the documents in his hand.

"Hang tight," he said before strutting back to his car.

Damn this lead foot of mine. I sat there patiently for about ten minutes before he came back to my window. Before he could say anything, I spoke first.

"First, Officer, I want to apologize for speeding on the highway like that. I don't know what I was thinking. I know that my actions were reckless, but I promise if you let me go...I will never speed again."

Smiling, he said, "So, you just rehearsed that while I was gone, huh? Nice touch Mrs. Stone, but you were going too fast to let you off with just a warning. You are my first stop of the day. I usually let my first stop off with a warning if I'm able to, but not this time. You've got to slow this thing down. You are going to kill yourself at this speed."

Not having the energy to spar, I agreed with him and took my ticket.

"Oh and if you don't mind me saying, you are far too beautiful to be crying this early in the morning. Is there anything I can do or say to ease your mind?" he asked.

"As a matter of fact there is. Pull my piece of shit husband over and brush up on your police brutality skills. That would truly make my day."

He cracked up laughing, grabbing at his side.

"Listen, Mrs. Stone. Unfortunately for you and lucky for him... I can't participate in purposely hurting someone. That goes against everything I believe. I know that law enforcement gets a bad rap but not all of us want to hurt people. Most of us, especially folks like me, just want to make it home safely."

"Make it home safely to your wife and kids?" I questioned as I raised my brows at him.

"Unfortunately, there is no wife and kids waiting for me. I'm very much single, Mrs. Stone. You take it easy and dry those tears. There is no man on this earth worth you crying for. You're beautiful, you're witty and I'm sure that you're a fantastic woman outside this car," he giggled. "Now drive safely."

"Will do, officer. Just so you know... I'm not paying this ticket. You all never show up at the courthouse on ticket day so it's going to be thrown out."

"Are you sure about that? You sound really sure, but I guess we just have to wait and see. Have a great day, beautiful," he said as he walked back to his car.

CHAPTER 4

1st Learn, 2nd Apply

I merged back onto the highway and continued my drive in silence. Arriving at my mother's house, I parked on the side of the road and sauntered to the front door. Sirus, my mother's cat, greeted me by brushing gently against my legs. Picking him up, I gave him cuddles before using my key and opening the door.

There she was, sitting on her couch watching *Judge Mathis*.

"Hey, Mama." I ran over to her and plopped down beside her. She put her tea down, grabbed and hugged me, then backed away.

"Zaya, I know damn well that man didn't put his hands on you. What is all that blood doing on your shirt?"

"Of course he didn't. I wouldn't be here if he did. I'd be in jail. I don't play that hitting stuff. Mama, I got so mad that my nose started to bleed. You remember how that would happen when I was little? It has started again, but I'm fine. I just need a shirt. Do you have one I could borrow?"

"I do, but hand me that one first. Let me put my little concoction on it and get that stain out. Then I'll throw it in the washer, and you can get it back before you leave. It won't take long."

"Thank you but wait. How about I give you everything I'm wearing and you wash it? I'd just come back from a run when all this went down, so I could use a nice hot shower and some fresh clean digs."

I stripped down and gave her all my clothes. She went in her room and gave me one of her muumuus. While she took my clothes to the washroom, I hopped in the shower. I came out fifteen minutes later feeling a tad better. It's amazing what hot water and your mama's presence can do for you. As soon as I sat down next to her, I broke down crying again.

She spun around toward me, grabbed my hand, and said, "It's gonna be okay, Zaya. I promise you it will. I know it hurts, but you will make it through. You've got to be strong for those babies. Those children deserve a whole mother, not a fractured one. Don't let that man knock you off your shit."

"I won't, Mama. You know I'm strong, but this right

here almost took me out. My heart is broken. Jhovan, Mama... Jhovan. I thought that he was one of the good ones. You know I built that man from scratch."

"Yes, sugar, I know you did, and that is half the problem. I told you a long time ago, never love a man more than he loves you. I also told you never pour more than what's being poured in your cup. Did you listen? No, you did not, and here we are. I don't want you to blame yourself because, as women, our job is to love and nurture and trust me, you are not to blame for his wayward dick. All I'm saying is if you didn't care so much, it wouldn't hurt as much."

"Mama, how do you share your life with somebody... be with them day in and day out and not love them too much? It's virtually impossible," I said, shrugging my shoulders.

"You're absolutely right. It's virtually impossible with your first husband, but not with your second." She winked at me.

"Explain please, Mama, because I think I'm a little confused," I admitted as I walked to the kitchen to pour myself a cup of tea.

"It's simple. First husband, learn. Second husband, apply."

"Mama, when I said I do, I only intended to say it one time," I chirped.

"Me too, but it didn't happen that way. I thought the sun rose and set on your father's hind parts, only to realize he was my test. My test to see if I'd learned what God tried to teach me. I didn't learn, and I failed. Just be patient, baby. He isn't done with you yet. Keep on living," she said softly before easing back on the couch.

"Mama, I'm not even going to pretend I know what you mean, and I don't have the mental fortitude right now to figure it out. I just know my heart hurts right now."

"So, are you staying or leaving him?"

"I don't know, Mama. I really don't. I don't want to throw away what we have, but I feel like he just did. He didn't consider me. He didn't consider my children. He didn't consider all that he stood to lose because of his actions."

"Child, they never do until it's too late. My advice is to make him stand on his word. Make him show you how much you mean to him. Make him show you how miserable his life would be without you. Make him suffer, baby. Make him crawl. He's got to prove it, not just say it."

"It's too soon to know how I'm going to handle this. I can't think clearly. What I do know is I wish that you knew voodoo. I'd make you turn his ass into a goat by midnight... then we could barbecue him for dinner tomorrow." I giggled.

She chuckled, grabbed my neck, and kissed my cheek.

"Zaya, your tail is crazy. Mama don't mess around with no witchery. All my gifts are heaven-sent. I do know one thing, though...the book of Psalms isn't anything to play with. That's all I'm going to say."

We sat quietly, exchanging smiles from time to time until I dozed off in her recliner. I woke up to her softly shaking my shoulder with my clothes in her hand.

"Zaya, baby, it's 1:45. Those kids get out at three, right? You need to get on up that road."

"Ok, Mama," I said, stretching and moving the throw from my legs. "Where is my stepfather? He should be home by now, shouldn't he?"

"Nawl, baby. Samson picked up extra shifts this month. We are planning a trip to the Maldives this summer. Somebody has got to pay for that," she chuckled, flashing that knowing grin.

"I know that's right, Mama," I said while getting dressed. I kissed her cheek, and she gave me the warmest hug.

"Oh, and I'm stealing this muumuu. It's so comfortable." Before she could say anything, I muttered, "I'll text you when I get back in town, and before you say it, yes, I will kiss your grandbabies and give them some sugar for you."

I left and took my time on the drive home. I called India to advise her that I was ready to work. She was so happy to hear it and advised that the business was being remodeled at the moment. As soon as they were back up and running, I would be the first she called. We discussed my salary and our goals for the company. After hanging up with India, I felt a bit better, especially knowing the salary would allow me to keep a house and my children fed if I decided to leave my piece-of-shit husband. Tears constantly tried to meet my cheeks, but they didn't have my permission. I refused to cry another tear. I told myself over and over to tighten up.

My head began to heat as I heard my mother's words replaying in my head: *"Your children deserve to have a whole mother... not a fractured one."*

With a lump in my throat, I pulled up at the school and smiled gently as they filed into the back seat. As Jhovan Jr. closed the back door, Jhovan called again, and his face appeared on the screen. I tried to ignore it and send him to voicemail before the kids noticed, but I wasn't fast enough.

"Mama, that's our daddy calling. Are you going to answer it?"

I ignored him and asked how everyone's day was going. Jhovan's face disappeared from the screen, and I breathed a sigh of relief.

"Good," they all said in unison.

"That's good, babies. Would you all like to go out to

eat tonight? Mama is tired, and I don't think I want to cook. How about we go for sushi? How does that sound?"

"Mama, now you know we love sushi," Trinity said, kicking her little feet.

"Sushi it is."

"Are you going to call Daddy to see if he'll be off work in time?" Jr. asked.

"I'm sure Daddy will be busy, baby. Maybe next time," I muttered as I continued driving. I wasn't quite ready to return home, so I took the children to the lake, which doubled as a park, to feed the ducks.

"Where are we going, Mama?" Thalia questioned.

"I was thinking we could go and feed the ducks, then we can stop for a little treat on the way home. How does that sound?"

They were excited and agreed. We pulled into the park, hopped out, and headed to the pavilion. I got a few quarters from my purse and gave one to each child. They ran to the grain dispenser, each waiting patiently to stick their little quarter in the machine. I sat on the bench while they stood in a single-file line. Thalia was in the back. She looked back at me, her face gleaming and smiling. I smiled back, and she began to wave and then ran toward me.

"Daddy! Daddy... where'd you come from? We are going to eat sushi tonight. Mama said she wasn't cooking.

Are you coming with us?" He picked her up, planting a big kiss on her cheek.

"Sure, I will. That's if your Mama doesn't mind. Mama's a little upset with Daddy. Daddy's been a little bad, but I'm hoping that your mother will forgive me."

This sick son of a bitch. I couldn't believe he would use our children to try and garner sympathy for himself. This muthafucka had no shame.

"So, Mama, what do you say? Can I have sushi with you and my babies?"

"Whatever you did, Daddy, I'm sure Mama will forgive you. Mama taught us not to hold grudges and to forgive. Isn't that right, Mama? Didn't you teach us that?" Thalia asked while she hugged her piece-of-shit father around the neck.

"That is indeed what I taught you. I guess Mama has to practice what she preaches, so yes, your father can come eat sushi with us."

Thalia cheered and kissed her father once again. I wanted to vomit, knowing those lips had been on someone else besides me.

"Go ahead and catch up with your brother and sister. You better run. The ducks will be full by the time you get there. Run, run, run." I cheered her on as she hopped out of Jhovan's arms.

As soon as she was an earshot's distance away, I turned

to Jhovan. "Don't you *ever* in your muthafuckin life put our children in the position to mediate for us. That is not their place. You be a grown man and talk to me directly. Never do that again, or I promise that I will cut your balls off and stuff them down your fucking throat." I scowled as I moved away from him.

"Zaya, please. Damn, that's a bit much, don't you think? I tried to talk to you directly, but you wouldn't answer the damn phone. I've been calling you all morning," he groaned.

"And? So what you've been calling? It's not like you didn't know that I was pissed. I'm mad, I'm angry, and I don't want to talk to your ass. Hell, I don't even want to breathe the same air as you. I don't want you here. Please get the fuck away from me," I yelled.

My voice echoed through the park. I turned around, and my babies were looking at me with confused looks on their faces. Bursting into tears, I ran back to my SUV. I could see the panic on Jhovan's face. I heard him tell our children that I was okay and he would come check on me.

I shook my head no when I saw him walking toward me. He kept walking. I shook my head no again. He continued toward me. I cranked my SUV and backed out. I got a mile up the road and called Jhovan.

"Hello, Zaya. Please don't leave like this, I'm so—"

"Put my children on the phone, please."

"Huh?"

"You heard me, Jhovan. Put my children on the phone," I repeated.

There was a long pause, then I heard him telling them to come to the phone.

"Mama, are you okay? Where did you go?" Jr. asked.

"I want all three of you to listen to me, okay? First, I am fine. I'm still a little upset about something that happened earlier, but it has nothing to do with you all. Daddy is going to take you to get sushi. I'm going to go off for a few hours, but I will be home later tonight. Mama just needs to cool off. I want you to go home and do any homework you have. If you have questions, your daddy can help you. Daddy is going to make sure that you bathe, get your clothes out for the morning, and put you all in the bed. Show him where everything is and how we do things. I love you all so very much, but Mama needs to see about herself right now. Do you all understand?"

"Yes, and okay, Mama. We love you," Trinity said.

"I love y'all too. Now, please give the phone back to your father."

"Zaya, I promise that all this isn't necessary. I told you that I would do whatever you ask." His voice was low and breathy.

"Go to hell. That's what you can do."

I hung up and called Pamela.

"Where are you, and when is your next break?"

"Ummm, hello to you too, bestie. I'm on 7th Street. Domestic disturbance, and I have an hour break at six. Is everything okay?"

"No, but it will be. Is the key to your place still on top of the light fixture?"

"It is. What's going on, Zaya?"

"Good. I'll be at your house. When you get a minute, stop by and see me," I instructed.

"Girl, you are scaring me. What in the hell is going on?" she sounded nervous.

"Nothing that a bottle can't fix. Do you have liquor at your house? You know what... never mind. You like brown. I want tequila, so I'll stop by the liquor store and get me a bottle. See ya later, bestie."

I hung up and made my way to the liquor store, where I picked up a bottle of Don Julio and headed to Pamela's house. My phone rang...my mother's face lit up the screen.

"Ooh, I'm so sorry, Mama. Don't fuss. I forgot to text you."

Scolding me, she said, "Yes, you did. I'll give you a pass because I know you've got shit going on, but don't let it happen again. You are my one and only. Don't have me over here worried about you."

"I won't, and there is no need to worry. I'm just fine. I love you, Mama."

"I love you too. Where are my grandchildren?"

"They are with their father. He's taking them to get sushi tonight."

"Ok. And?"

"And what, Mama?"

"And you aren't with them? That man never takes those babies anywhere without you. His ass probably doesn't even know how to load them into the car."

"Well, it's time for some things to change. I have to go. I'll call you later. I love you. Bye." I didn't give her the chance to ask another question or make another statement. I hung up and sped across town to Pamela's condo.

I grabbed my things and exited the car before discreetly retrieving the key from the light fixture. The smell of hibiscus and laundry detergent smacked me in the nose. I rounded the corner, and there was Ross standing there with a laundry basket full of dirty clothes.

"Oh shit, Ross. You scared the shit out of me. What are you doing here?"

"Oh, hey, Zaya. I just came by to do laundry. The washing machine at my mama's house went out, so I brought all our stuff over here to take care of it," he muttered while transferring clothes to the dryer.

"Umm, does... does Pamela know that you are here?"

"Nawl, she doesn't, but I'm sure she won't mind."

A bitter laugh left my throat.

"Did you talk to her today?" My head involuntarily tilted to the side.

"I haven't today, but we talked last night. She called me this morning, but I wasn't up yet. I figured whatever she needed that early in the morning could wait."

I sucked my teeth before taking my Don Julio out of the bag, breaking the seal, and taking a swig.

"Well, Ross, I wouldn't be so sure that she'd be okay with you being over here. If I were you, I'd call her ASAP," I snickered.

"Yo, Zaya, what in the fuck is so funny?" His voice raised with a touch of anger. He was annoyed; I could tell, but I didn't give a shit.

"First of all, Ross, don't curse at me. Today is not the muthafuckin day. I promise you this ain't what you want."

"What is your bougie ass gonna do?" he scowled. "You ain't gon' do shit."

I laughed again, this time out of disbelief, because who in the hell was he talking to? I took another swig. By now, I could feel it in my toes. I put the bottle down and reached in my purse, grabbing my nine.

"Don't let this sweet face fool you, bitch. I may live in the suburbs now, but I was born and raised in the hood. Are you sure you want to fuck with me today? Huh, Ross? Are you sure that this was the day that you wanted to fuck with Zaya?" I pointed the gun at his toes and giggled.

"Nawl, lil mama, you got it. Umm... umm... I... I'm just gonna roll. I'll come back later for my shit."

"Yeah, that's what I thought, 'cause who in the fuck you feeling like?"

I picked the bottle back up and took another swig. Before I could utter another word, he was out the door. I hollered laughing.

I sent Pamela a text message.

> Me: Just wanted you to know that I made it to your place. I also wanted you to know that Ross was in here washing a year's worth of clothes.

> Pamela: Wtf you mean he was in my place? He doesn't have a key.

> Me: Well, he was here, and your spare key was where you usually keep it. It could only mean that he had a key made.

> Pamela: Shit... how did you get him out of there? He's stubborn as hell, so I know he didn't just leave.

> Me: Umm, Mrs. Officer... we will talk about that later, lol.

> Pamela: Oh shit. Zaya, what did you do?

I didn't respond. Instead, I grabbed my bottle and plopped down on her couch. Taking another swig, I grabbed the remote and turned to *Tubi* to find a ratchet movie to watch.

Five shots in, and I started to get a little hungry. I already knew there was nothing to eat in Pamela's kitchen. She was barely home, and cooking was not her ministry. I hurriedly called the pizza joint up the street and had a large sausage and pepperoni delivered.

The tequila was hitting hard at this point, and I needed a little grease to help me out. On top of being tipsy, I developed the *itis* and dozed off.

CHAPTER 5

Hey Mr. Officer

"Zaya," Pamela yelled. "Wake your ass up."

She scared me so bad, I nearly jumped out of my skin. I still had the bottle in one hand and a slice of pizza in the other.

"Oh, hey girl..." I chirped while wiping marinara sauce from my mouth. "Is it 6:00 already?"

"Actually, it's 6:30. I got tied up at work. Never mind that. What in the hell do you have going on? I've never seen you like this...half-empty bottle of tequila, slouched over on the couch wearing a damn Lululemon outfit. Now tell me what is going on."

"What's going on is, I need to go get the same test that you just got to make sure I don't have anything. Jhovan is cheating on me," I admitted, rubbing my fingers through my hair.

NO LONGER YOURS

"Oh my God, Zaya. I'm so sorry. Did he confess or something? Did you have one of your dreams? How'd you find out?"

"I was having dreams but that's all they were. That was until the nasty heifer mailed her funky-ass panties to my house along with a letter. Girl, this morning was a mess. I don't feel like talking about it. As a matter of fact... I don't want to feel anything, which is why this bottle is coming in clutch."

"I understand. I won't ask you anything else about Jhovan. You know this is a one-bedroom, but you're welcome to sleep with me or on the couch if you prefer," she said empathetically as she sat down beside me.

"No, boo. I'm good. I'm going home. I just needed time to process."

"And this is how you chose to process, huh? A bottle of liquor and pizza?"

"Yeah, and what about it? It's better than doing what I wanted to do, which would have ended with me in hand-cuffs before night's end. I think this is a much better way of handling things."

"You know what, Zaya... you're right. Now tell me how you got Ross to leave."

I lifted the pillow where I had my gun tucked. "There she is. I told him to get the fuck on, or I was going

❀ 53 ❀

to *Harlem Nights* his pinkie toe, and he hauled ass." I laughed.

"Zaya!!! Are you telling me you pulled a gun on him?" She covered her mouth, trying to stifle her giggles.

"I may have," I blushed.

"Girl, you are too damn much. Anyway, I can't stay long. I just wanted to come by and check on you. I've got to get back to work, but I'll be off at nine. Will you still be here?"

"Not sure. Maybe, maybe not," I shrugged.

"Well, at least promise me that you won't leave here until you sober up. I don't want to have to arrest my best friend for drunk driving."

"I don't want you to have to arrest me either," I grinned and kissed her on the cheek.

She got up, grabbed her gear, and walked out the door. I waited about ten minutes after she'd left and decided it was best if I just went home. Before I walked out the door, I sent Jhovan a text.

> Me: I'm coming home in a few. I do not want to deal with you or talk about today's events. I just want to take a bath and go to bed without you being in it. Please sleep in the guestroom until I can figure out my next move. I don't need a response. Just your cooperation.

Jhovan: I'm just glad you're coming home. I will do whatever you want me to. I will be in the guestroom if you need me.

I looked down at the phone, scowling, and sauntered out of Pamela's condo.

I hopped in my ride and started up the road, deciding to take the short way home. I got on the highway only to realize that my vision was a tad bit blurred, and shit kept moving in front of me. I thought I'd slept it off enough to drive home without hurting myself or others, but I was wrong. I pulled over on the highway to sober up a little. I put on my hazards, which was a bad idea because, within five minutes, a state trooper was once again walking up to my car.

"Well, Mrs. Stone. If it isn't your pretty face again. What are you doing on the side of the road? Do you need me to call Triple-A?"

"No, officerrrrr...?"

"It's Officer Williams," he said.

"Officer Williams. Oh, that's right. That was the name on the ticket you graciously blessed a sad and crying woman with this morning," I slurred.

"Mrs. Stone... are you drunk?"

"A little bit, but that is why I'm on the side of the road. I had a few drinks earlier. I thought I was okay, but the more I drove, the more I realized that I was not okay, so I pulled over to sober up."

"You have no idea how much I appreciate you for doing that. I wish others thought to do the same. Technically, I'm supposed to still arrest you because you are inebriated behind the wheel of a car, but I'm not going to do that."

He sighed and looked at me for a long second, his flashlight lowering from my face to the gravel. "I'm not going to arrest you," he repeated. "But I can't just leave you out here either."

He opened my door and held out his hand. "Come on, let's get you some air."

I hesitated but took it. His palm was warm; his grip was firm but careful. I stumbled out and leaned against the side of the car while the night air hit me. It was sharp and cold, slicing through the fog in my head. It was just what I needed.

"Sit here," he said, guiding me to the hood of his cruiser. "You need some water." He went to the passenger side and came back with a cold bottle, cracking the seal before handing it to me.

I took it and smiled crookedly. "You always this nice to drunk women?"

He chuckled, the sound low and smooth. "Only the

honest ones. Most of y'all try to convince me you just had a sip of wine two hours ago."

I laughed, almost choking on the water. "Honesty gets me far, huh?"

"It got you out of handcuffs," he teased. "So I'd say yes."

He leaned back on the hood next to me, arms crossed, his gaze drifting to the empty stretch of highway ahead. For a moment, we sat in silence with only the sound of passing cars in the distance.

"I'm sorry," I muttered. "For... being a mess."

He glanced at me, his tone softening. "You're not a mess, Mrs. Stone. You're someone trying to hold it together. There's a difference."

That hit harder than it should have. I looked down at the bottle in my hands, twisting the cap. "It's been a long day."

"I believe that," he said quietly. "But you don't need someone who pushes you to this point. Whatever's going on in your life... no one's worth drinking yourself sick over."

My chest tightened, his words hitting heavy, but I didn't want to show it. "You don't even know me."

He smiled slightly, eyes meeting mine. "I know pain when I see it. And I know a woman who's trying too hard to look strong."

I turned away before he could see the flood sitting in my eyes. "You sound like my husband. He used to talk to me like that... before things got complicated."

"Then he must've had good sense at one point," he said with a half-smirk. "But if he's the reason you're sitting out here half-drunk and half-broken, then he forgot who he had."

After about thirty minutes, he helped me back to my car. "You're not driving far," he said firmly. "I'll follow you home. Just keep it slow. If you start to drift, I'll pull you over again, and this time you're riding with me. Deal?"

"Yes, sir," I whispered, sobering fast.

He grinned. "You 'yes, sir' me now, but five minutes ago I was 'Officer Williams, the man who blessed you with a ticket.'"

I couldn't help but laugh. "You caught that, huh?"

"Oh, I caught it. You're a handful."

When we got to my driveway, he stayed behind me, lights dimmed, until I stepped out. I tried to wave but stumbled, catching myself on the car door. Before I could hit the ground, his hands were there. Firm and steady.

"Whoa, whoa," he said, helping me stand upright. "You good?"

"Yeah," I said softly. "Thank you... for not judging me."

His eyes softened. "I'm not here to judge you, Zaya. Just to make sure you make it home safe."

Hearing my name in his voice did something to me. Something I didn't want to admit.

He stepped back toward his cruiser, then looked over his shoulder. "Get some rest. And tomorrow? Maybe be a little kinder to yourself. You're too beautiful to let pain win."

I stood there long after he drove off, my heart pounding in my chest.

When I finally made it upstairs, I sat on the edge of the bed, staring at the wall. I thought about his words. His hands. His calm. How he made me feel seen when I'd spent all day feeling invisible.

And then I thought about Jhovan... how he used to take care of me like that. How he'd hold me when I cried, how he'd run a bath or make me tea. How it used to feel to be loved like that.

Now, it just felt like an ache I couldn't shake.

I curled up under the blanket, the house quiet, my mind still replaying his voice. *You're too beautiful to let pain win.*

With his words and beautiful face in mind, I let my hands roam until they found a spot to soothe. My throbbing clit needed some much-needed attention, and I wouldn't dare deny myself the simple pleasure. I licked my fingers and slid them down to my center, gently circling my clit. I imagined tasting his lips and him tasting mine. I reached under my bed to grab my dildo... by now, I was soaking wet and aching for some pressure. I sucked the tip before plunging it deep into my yoni. I moaned quietly as I stroked my pussy and circled my nipples.

Hopping up on my knees, I held it in place and rode the dick like a champ. The whole time, I imagined it was his. My pussy was so wet, it damn near disappeared and got lost. My hand was soaked from my juices, but I wasn't done. I rolled over on my side and slid it in from the back, fucking myself into an oblivion. I came so hard, I caught a charley horse that fucked up my whole euphoric feeling. Guess that's what I got for thinking about fucking on another man while my husband was in another room. After the pain subsided, I cleaned myself up and hopped back into bed.

I smiled to myself just a little before drifting off. Finally feeling seen. Not by the man who broke me... but by a stranger who cared enough to help me home. And when sleep finally came, it was his voice I heard. It was calm, patient, telling me I was worth saving.

That Day

The next month or so was rough. I struggled with forgiving him but eventually ended up caving. I didn't want to end our relationship because of one mistake. He wasn't perfect, and neither was I. I was reminded of that when I strutted into that court-house excited to see Officer Williams, only to discover that I had no ticket to pay. It had been taken care of, and I was free to go. Him not showing up was a sign that I didn't need to see him anyway. The way my heart thumped at the thought of that man couldn't be good for my marriage either.

Jhovan and I made the decision to attend counseling, and we did so twice a week. We enacted mandatory date nights and actively listened to each other. I set appoint-ments, and we both were tested for every disease imagin-

❧ 61 ❧

able. They all came back negative. He started being romantic again and seemed to really try his hardest to regain my trust. There were no more boxes on my front porch, and everything seemed to be going great.

That was until that day.

That day started out like any other. I woke up at 5:00 A.M., started a pot of coffee, cranked up the music, and then I sauntered off to each of our little one's rooms to begin our morning routine. Cuddles and smiles while I sang them gently out of their slumber. A few tickles and prayers always followed. We always thanked God for another day.

Then, I helped them wash their faces and brush their teeth before preparing them a nutritious breakfast. Then I trekked off to my bathroom to brush my teeth, take a shower, and get myself together. After getting dressed, feeding everyone and making sure they were good, I grabbed my coffee, loaded everyone in the SUV and dropped them off at school — all while he was asleep.

Each morning, I completed this same routine, and of the fourteen years that I'd been married to the nasty, trifling, self-serving son of a bitch, not one morning did he assist with any of it. I guess by this point he thought he was bigger than the program. I probably helped shape his thought process because for years, I treated him like the king he pretended to be.

After I was done dropping the kids off, I stopped by his favorite French bakery to grab his go-to... a chocolate éclair donut and iced coffee. Then I returned home to iron his work clothes, make his lunch, and finish planning my day. Although the day started off just like any other, it most definitely didn't end that way.

Stepping back into my home, I was greeted with silence, which was odd because by now, Jhovan would usually be up and moving around. I ascended the stairs to hear the shower running, but with a closer ear, I could tell no one was in it. He'd left the bathroom door cracked just enough for me to see him posted up against the sink, smiling and laughing like a love-sick schoolgirl. After I'd witnessed enough of the bullshit, I finally called out.

"Hey, Jhovan, what in the hell are you in there sniggling and giggling about? Shouldn't you be in the shower? You're going to be late for work," I spat.

Quickly hanging up the phone, he stepped out of the bathroom. "Oh, hey babe. I didn't know you were back. How is your morning going so far?"

Cutting my eyes at him, I murmured, "It's going just fine. I see you were in there on a call, and from the smile on your face, the conversation had to be exciting... Do tell, Jhovan. I want to laugh too."

He rolled his eyes and snapped, "Come on now, Zaya. Please don't start tripping. That was just my mama. She called me just as I was about to get into the shower. She wanted to know if we were coming to the family reunion this year. I told her the only way we would show up is if it were somewhere inside this time. Last time we almost burned up out there. I think she keeps forgetting that this is Florida, and the heat isn't shit to play with." He searched my face to see if I was buying it.

I wasn't, but I had no proof that he was lying, so I smiled and muttered, "I'm glad you told her because if you didn't, I would have. She should know by now that I don't do the heat... or bugs. If she wants us to come, she better figure something else out besides that tired-ass park she's always renting out. Hell, as much as she charges for the dues, she could at least rent out somewhere with central air. With her cheap ass," I giggled.

"Hey, hey, hey, don't be talking about my mama. You know she hates the word cheap. She prefers to be called frugal or money savvy. Whatever in the hell that means."

"Yeah, whatever, Jhovan. Go on and hop in the shower. You are wasting precious resources. I'm sure that if your mother were here, she'd be having a conniption right now."

"You're right," he said as he shuffled over to me and kissed my forehead before stripping and leaving his clothes in the middle of our bedroom floor.

"So baby, what do you have on your itinerary for today?" He yelled from the bathroom.

I ignored his question and gathered up the clothes he'd left in the middle of the floor. The scent of her hit me first... that same cheap-ass smell from the gift box. It was the kind of perfume that pretends to be classy but clings like desperation. My chest tightened. I held his shirt to my nose, just to be sure.

It wasn't mine. My shit was $297.00 a bottle. My skin could never.

He was still in the shower, singing like nothing was wrong... much like last time... that same off-key hum he used to get on my nerves. I felt something cold crawl down my spine, and for the first time in fourteen years, I didn't push it away. I let it sit, settle, and bloom.

I crept back into the bathroom while his back was turned and grabbed his phone. Quietly, I closed the door before sitting on the bed. I stared at it for a few seconds before taking the leap and facing the truth.

He never locked it. He was too arrogant, too sure I'd never get the inkling. I don't know why in the fuck he thought that. At the end of the day... I was still a woman.

I scrolled through his texts until I saw the name "Canada Wet ."

The audacity.

My blood ran cold as the messages flashed before my

eyes... photos, emojis, videos of him giving a beautiful, statuesque, caramel skinned woman back shots. Of her with her lips wrapped around the dick that I'd said vows to. Messages containing words he hadn't said to me in years. Compliments I used to dream of hearing again. "I miss you." "Can't wait to taste you." "You're my peace."

His peace.

I stared at those words until my hands trembled. I'd been breaking my back for this man, loving him through every lie, holding our family together while he gave our pieces away to someone else.

A pain rippled through my chest.

I walked to the bathroom door and watched him through the steam. He was rinsing his hair, still humming, still free. I thought about the prayers I'd said with my babies that morning. About how I'd thanked God for this life... this lie.

He looked up, caught my reflection in the mirror, and smiled. "Babe, you okay?"

I smiled back, slow and steady. "Never better." But inside, something cracked. Not small. Not fixable. Something that screamed... he'd fucked with the wrong one.

Because the moment I saw her name, I stopped being his peace—and started becoming his punishment.

In a hurry, I grabbed my phone and screen-recorded everything I could. Luckily for me, he loved taking long showers, but unlucky for him, it gave me more than enough time to plunder. The more I saw, the more fury coursed through my veins.

The rest of that morning, I was on autopilot. Once he was done with his shower, he dressed and kissed me goodbye like nothing in the world had changed. And I let him.

I stood in the doorway and watched him pull out of the driveway. His coffee in the cup holder, his favorite éclair on the seat beside him, and my heart on ice. I waited until the sound of his tires faded, then I locked the door and let the silence swallow me whole. My body trembled. First, sadness overwhelmed me, then in the blink of an eye, it disappeared and was replaced with something colder. A calculating certainty that he had to get his. He had to pay.

I'd given him three beautiful children and fourteen years of blind loyalty... fourteen years of giving him everything, my youth, my time, my body, my forgiveness.

All while he drained me, one lie at a time.

I walked back upstairs, still barefoot, the cool floor grounding me. His scent lingered. The expensive cologne I'd bought for our anniversary hung in the air, mixed with the stale, cheap floral scent of her perfume on his shirt. I sat on the edge of the bed and stared at my phone.

Every message, every photo, every "I love you" felt like a dare. He didn't even bother to delete them. That's when it hit me... he didn't give a damn. He didn't fear losing me. He didn't love me, and he for damn sure didn't respect me. And *that*... was his first mistake.

I started scanning through screenshots, notes, time-stamps. I ran to the copier and printed copies of our bank statements and phone records. Scoured through the messages and discovered it wasn't just one... but three. One of them wasn't even old enough to legally take a sip of alcohol. Fucking pervert.

My fingers stopped trembling, and my breathing slowed. I'd been emotional for years. Now it was time to become surgical.

I opened the window to let the morning light in. The birds were chirping. The world was still beautiful.

And for the first time today, an eerie calm covered me like a blanket.

Maybe because the difference between a woman scorned and a woman awakened...is strategy.

I wasn't going to scream, cry, or beg him to explain himself. I was going to ruin him. Slowly and silently. And when I was done, he'd look back on this day and wish that his mammie would have swallowed him instead.

I poured myself another cup of coffee and made my way to the couch. There I sat for hours staring at the phone.

How?

How did he pull the wool over my eyes for so long? Some of those messages went back years, and I never knew.

But more than the how, I wanted the why and deep down, I knew I'd never get it.

Even if he confessed and laid his every sin bare, there was no way I would believe him. His words meant shit to me now, and this kind of betrayal I couldn't move past. Heaviness sat in my chest as this realization came into clarity.

There wasn't a therapist on earth that could convince me to stay with someone who could and would do the things he'd done. The more I thought about it, the more pissed I became.

Jhovan had some fucking nerve. When I met him, he was a fat, pudgy, nerdy muthafucka whose idea of a good time was collecting Pokémon cards and playing cornhole in his mother's backyard. Every ounce of sexiness he possessed was inspired by me. I told him I needed him healthy. We would eventually have a family one day, and I needed him to stick around for our children to be. He agreed, and I signed us both up for gym memberships.

For three years straight, I cooked only healthy food and meal-prepped weekly to help him stay on track.

His swag? All me.

A college friend turned celebrity stylist took Jhovan on his first designer shopping trip, my favor. This was where I helped him curate his style and taught him how to choose clothing that would fit well with his body type.

My best friend's brother was a superb barber, and I convinced him to cut that bird's nest he called hair off his head and get a tight Caesar fade. This elevated his look to the max. It's amazing what a haircut can do for a man.

We traded those glasses in for contacts, and I even bought the bastard a $100.00 beard oil to aid in turning that dreadful patch on his face into a full-on Philly beard. And after all that, this is the thanks I get. Before me, Jhovan was just existing. Because of me, he was living.

I not only helped him with his physical but his mental. I poured into him just as a wife should. I never wanted my husband to wonder where he stood with me, so I constantly reassured him in any way he required. I told and showed him how much I appreciated him. We prayed together, and I would let him hear me thanking God for bringing him into my life. Jhovan worked as a foreman, but I convinced him to get his general contractor's license so he could stop working for others and start a business for himself.

I lost count of the nights I stayed up helping him study for his exam. When he passed with flying colors, I threw a party to celebrate his accomplishments. I was always celebrating him, yet I couldn't think of the last time he'd celebrated me.

All in all, I'd been his ride-or-die and backbone, and he turned around and cheats on me.

Me.

I'm the best thing that ever happened to his ass. He should have been grateful my mother taught me to look within and not the outside appearance. Otherwise, the bastard wouldn't have stood a chance.

His Representative

Jhovan and I met on a blind date set up by my former friend and ex-coworker, Sylvia. Sylvia always went on and on about her boyfriend's roommate, saying that I should meet him, and she thought we'd be great for each other. I turned down her offer time and time again because, at this point in my life, I wasn't looking for anything serious. I'd just graduated college and was trying to get myself together. I'd worked hard for my degree, and I wanted to focus on building my career and clientele.

My goal was to become an interior decorator to the stars, and I sure as hell couldn't do that if I didn't get off my ass and go for it. I bagged a gig in Destin, Florida, staging homes and helping with layouts for renovations. The area was booming with new construction and was right up the street from one of the largest Air Force bases in the world.

It was also home to some of the most beautiful white, sandy beaches around. Destin wasn't my dream location, California was, but it would do until I could snag the bigger contracts and relocate. I was as free as a bird...no children, no man, and nothing to hold me back or down. Sylvia helped me get familiar with the area, and for that, I was grateful. But when it came to dating? My luck was trash. I kept running into the same kind of men. Married military guys who appeared single but had a whole wife and family at home. They all wanted the same thing... a side piece.

I wasn't going for that shit. I wasn't about to be second or third to anyone. The ones who weren't married were usually gay and looking for a beard, and that surely wouldn't work for me. I needed to be the only one in my relationship requiring dick.

After one too many failed encounters, Sylvia suggested again that I go on a blind date with her boyfriend's room-mate, Jhovan. I only agreed to go out with him because I was tired of spending nights in my apartment twiddling my thumbs. I needed some excitement.

The beach had gotten old... I would come home with sand in places I never imagined, and it was wreaking havoc on my skin. I needed a change of scenery. I wanted to have some fun, experience something new. When Sylvia asked again, I finally agreed. Sylvia made reservations at one of the nicest restaurants in town. The kind of place you couldn't just stroll into wearing jeans and a T-shirt. I rummaged through the closet of my tiny apartment and found the nicest digs I owned, a cute cocktail dress with four-inch pumps.

I was 23 at the time. Wrinkle-free, with smooth milk chocolate skin, long kinky coils, a tiny waist, thick and curvy in all the right places, with an ass big as Texas. I knew what I was working with, and to me... I was a big deal.

I decided to drive myself instead of letting him pick me up. There was no way I was letting a stranger know where I lived. Sylvia had given me a vague description of Jhovan. She described him as a dark-skinned cutie with a little fluff. Sylvia told me he would be easy to spot because he had a distinct beauty mark on his cheek.

I strutted in and was promptly seated. Within five minutes, the pudgy, mole-faced fucker sat down in front of me. My first instinct was to laugh, not because he was ugly, because he wasn't. He just wasn't what I expected. That beauty mark Sylvia mentioned? Yeah, it was a full-on mole with a piece of hair hanging out of it.

I wasn't a shallow person by any means, but I had a type, and he wasn't it. I knew within seconds this would be our first and last date, but I figured I'd stay for the free dinner. To my surprise, Jhovan turned out to be extremely charming. He was smart, ambitious, and had a great sense of humor. I was goofy as hell, and laughter was one of the quickest ways to my heart.

During our time at the restaurant, he kept me entertained and giggling the entire time. By the end of dinner, the "one and done" date turned into two. Two turned into three. Before I knew it, we were engaged and married within two years of meeting each other.

Jhovan wanted a big family and expressed his desire to start having kids right away. I wanted to travel the world and put some stamps in my passport first. I promised to give him a namesake after we'd visited all the places I'd dreamed of. We began traveling immediately, and within five years, our passports were full. He kept every promise he'd made, and so did I.

At twenty-eight, I gave him his first child, a beautiful little boy named after his father. A year later came Thalia, and two years after that, Trinity. My hands were full and my hands alone. Jhovan clearly enjoyed making babies, but caring for them was a different subject. With me, he was so attentive. He catered to my every need, and I assumed it would be the same with our children. I was so wrong.

Neither of us knew anything about kids, but only one of us was eager to learn. His idea of being a good father was coming home, kissing them on the forehead, and heading off to do his own thing. All the household duties and caring for the kids fell solely upon me.

Jhovan was the type of husband who thought the extent of him taking care of his family lied strictly in paying the bills. In his mind, as long as he was providing, he was doing his part. I was essentially a married single parent. Sadly, I saw this with a lot of fathers...including my own...but that was another story for another day.

After hours of sifting through memories, plundering, reflecting, and asking questions I'd never get the answer to, I got up and began cleaning my house from top to bottom. Cleaning usually helped clear my mind but didn't seem to work this time. My head was throbbing, and I was exhausted from thinking and wondering. I wanted to start plotting but that would have to wait. I didn't have the mental capacity to dream up anything solid, so I promised myself I would play it cool and act as if nothing was wrong.

I knew this would be difficult for me because I'd never been the type of person to hold in my grievances. However, if I wanted to walk away with the upper hand, I would have to play this thing cool. Calculated was the word of the day, hell the year. This would require playing the long game.

For fourteen years, I'd been the good wife to that bastard, and for seven of those years, I'd been unhappy.

That was no more. I decided the minute I opened that phone and discovered his truth, I would start living in mine. Being with him wasn't what I wanted anymore. His mask started falling off years ago and I needed to get away from him. From the lies. From the deceit. It had to be done right, though. I would have to take the emotions out of it and be methodical. I would have to become him, a selfish, self-serving piece of shit and I was going to enjoy my transformation.

I could not let him see me unravel. He'd taken enough from me already. I wasn't going to hand over my sanity. So, when I heard the garage door lift and his heavy footsteps echo through the hallway, I took one last deep breath, forcing my face into something that resembled peace. I even practiced the smile, soft, patient, and loving. The kind of smile that said everything's fine, even though everything inside me was screaming.

"Hey, baby," he said, dropping his keys on the counter like he always did. "Did you cook? Cause I'm starving."

Taking in a deep breath, I turned slowly, a dish towel in my hand, and met his eyes with that same smile. "Of course I did. I made marry me chicken. Your favorite." My voice was calm; it was honey sweet. But inside, I wanted to bash his skull with the cast iron skillet I'd just set on the stove.

He smiled, oblivious to the storm churning within.

"Hell yeah, Zaya. You know just what I like. You the shit, girl."

"Mmm-hmmm," I hummed, walking past him. I brushed his arm lightly, the way a loving wife would. My hand tingled with restraint. I could feel my pulse pounding in my fingertips. This was going to be so hard. I should fuck him up, standing over there smiling at me, looking like who done it and what for. I wondered, did he smile at those bitches like that?

He didn't notice the shift in me; men like him rarely do. They get so used to you bending that they don't realize when you've actually broke.

I set the table, called the kids to come eat. I fixed everyone's plate, and we sat down to eat as a family. We talked about his day; the kids and I laughed at his tired-ass jokes, and as painful as it was, I kept a smile on my face. Every movement and every word was perfectly measured. But behind my teeth, behind my pretty smile, was an evil brewing that no one was ready for.

After the plates were cleared and the kids were down for the night, the house finally folded into that low hum of ordinary life...a thermostat click, the distant inaudible voice on the television, a child's muffled laugh down the hall.

Jhovan flopped onto the couch, half-listening to the

game playing on the screen, scratching at his jaw like he owned the calm in the room.

I stood in the kitchen, hands on the sink, watching him like I was studying a blueprint I'd drawn myself. He looked exactly like the man I'd made: wide shoulders from years of ease, confident because I'd taught him to be, comfortable because I let him be. I felt a terrible, cold pride at that. I had built this man from a boy who'd once needed my directions to a man who took what he wanted and called it destiny. I'd styled him, fed his ego, smoothed every rough edge I found until he fit the life I wanted. And now? Now I would unbuild him.

"Zay?" he asked, glancing up. "Are you okay?"

"I'm fine, love," I said softly, measured. "I've just got a lot on my mind... that's all. I'm going to bed early. It's been a long day."

"Don't be too early. I'm going to come up there and put you to sleep. Just give big daddy a few minutes. The game is almost over."

With my shoulders sagging, I headed upstairs.

"Wait, Zay. Where are you going?"

"I just told you I was going to bed early. I was serious. I'm about to shut it down for the night."

"I know where you're going, but where is my sugar? Gimme some love, girl."

This was it. This was the part I hadn't considered. He

thought we were good. He had no idea that I was seething underneath this fake-ass smile. He wanted some affection, some pussy, and I wanted to filet his dick and butterfly his balls. I guess tonight, neither would get what we wanted.

"I think I'm coming down with a cold, baby," I spoke. "I don't want you to get sick. I'll head to the drugstore tomorrow, but tonight, I just want to sleep."

"I'm sorry, Zaya. I didn't know that you weren't feeling good. Is there anything that I could do to make you feel better?"

He really didn't want to know the answer to that, so I simply muttered, "Let me go lie down. That's what you can do."

"Okay, well, I'll leave you alone. I'll wait for that sweet sugar of yours for years if I have to. I just want you to feel better."

"Uhh-huh," I said as I shuffled up the stairs. I took a shower and climbed into bed, thinking of all the ways I would ruin him and I wouldn't wait forever to start either.

This night, my dream wasn't of Jhovan and his little sluts. I dreamed of Officer Williams, those dimples, the soft hands, the kind smile, and the body that looked as if he worked out seven days a week. That was the only thing that invaded my dreams, and I woke up determined to catch up with him again.

The next morning after dropping the kids off at

school, I phoned Pamela before heading to her house. She opened the door looking like she had been fucked six ways from Sunday.

"Girl, what the hell do you want this early in the morning?"

"I want a favor from my best friend. Don't worry, it doesn't involve you doing any kind of unethical shit this time. I need you to find this fine ass state troopers phone number for me. His name is Officer Williams. Can you do that without giving me any lip? Also, can you explain to me why you have that freshly fucked look on your face?"

She waved me off as she turned around and headed to her kitchen to start a pot of coffee. "Well, Zaya, if you must know... I had company last night. She just left ten minutes ago."

"Wait a minute, heifer. You dipping in the lady pool now?"

"I am. Is that a problem?"

"Not at all. I mean, I've known you forever and never knew you to be into girls. You know I don't do any judging, so if you like it... I love it."

"Good, 'cause I'd hate to have to curse you out this early in the morning. Hell, I'm too tired anyway. Now, why do you need that man's number? I thought you and your husband were working it out?"

"He's working it out. I'm working on moving on.

That bastard is still cheating, and he has no idea that I know. I'm going to keep it like that. I want him none the wiser. Now, I didn't come here to talk about his ass. I came here to get that fine-ass officer's information so that I can get up with him. We've got some things to talk about." I popped my lips as I flashed her a knowing smile.

"I'm on the evening shift today. I should have it by the time you get off. Now, I'm doing you this favor...what are you going to do for me, bestie?"

"I'm not putting my lips on your pussy if that's what you're asking." We looked at each other and cracked up laughing. "'Cause I don't do any munching. I'm the one getting munched on."

She chuckled and shook her head as she poured herself a cup of coffee.

"No seriously, Zaya. I want you to be careful, and if you are going to be doing any illegal shit over there, don't tell me. I don't want to know shit."

"Got it. Thank you for your services, and I'll talk to you later. I've got errands to run," I winked at her as I walked out the front door.

CHAPTER 8

His Undoing

I headed to Walmart, then GNC, to pick up a few things to get my sabotage on. I would destroy him from the crown down. I started with Nair, pre-workout and post-workout powder, weight gain powder, turpentine, estrogen, and thumbtacks.

I stopped to get his favorite dessert. Chocolate éclair doughnuts. Eight in one box for my children and four in another box for him alone. After the loot had been secured, I headed home. Jhovan went to work and so did I. Getting out my piping kit, I mixed cream cheese, sugar, a little vanilla, and weight gain powder...700 calories per scoop. Then, piped it into each doughnut, put a little ribbon and card on the box, and voilà, a fat fucker starter kit.

Afterward, I ran upstairs to the bathroom to seek out

his shampoo and body wash. I poured Nair into the bottles, shook it up, and put it back on the counter. I rambled through the cabinets for my old progesterone tablets. Since he was acting like a bitch, I was going to turn him into a real one. I opened the capsules, poured the contents into the pill bottle to use later on in his meals and drinks. I poured out 85% of the expensive imported beard oil and replaced it with turpentine and safflower oil, which was known to slow down hair growth.

Once everything was set in place, I turned on my stereo and put on my 2000s crunk playlist. I started with "Knuck If You Buck." Loud bass flooded every corner of my house. I was going bar for bar as I opened his laptop to his bid estimates. I changed a few numbers in each column, as well as the addresses, and closed it back. The day I rambled through his phone, I'd made sure to screenshot and jot down the phone numbers and names of each slut. I'd done my research and found out where they lived, as well as their employers. I also found their accounts on Sniffer.com.

That's where he found the nasty bitch that left her funky, cheesy-ass panties on my porch and one other. The other woman wasn't a woman at all. She was a young naive college student. I decided to leave her alone because, from her messages, she had no idea he was married. I would save her dignity but I would show the other sluts no mercy.

Ms. Canada Wet, whose real name was Solee, was originally from Ontario. Hence the name Canada Wet. She was a night nurse at a prestigious private Catholic hospital in our area. Sending an email to her boss, I advised that she'd violated HIPAA laws by discussing patients with others. I emailed them screenshots of her and Jhovan poking fun at the size of a patient's penis while the patient was under anesthesia.

She was dumb enough to take a picture of the patient and send it to Jhovan. I sent the photo along with a video of her fucking my husband in a utility closet at work. The stupid bitch's badge and ID were in the pic clear as day. I also advised them of her profile on Sniffer.com.

The other bitch, Calliope, was a schoolteacher. He had videos of her giving him head inside her classroom. I sent that video to the principal along with her Sniffer profile details. Her profile stated she was a naughty teacher that loved to punish the naughtiest students. This dimwit had pictures on her profile of her grading actual papers from one of the kids in her class. I zoomed in and quoted the students' names in the email. I sent the same photos, videos, and email to her husband of seventeen years, and a copy to the church email where her father was the pastor.

I decided I'd done enough for the day and was satisfied with myself. Now all that was left to do was sit back and watch the carnage.

When Jhovan sauntered into the house after work, I could tell he wasn't in the best of moods. He dared not ask me about anything, though, because that would be admittance. Men like him didn't admit shit because they were cowards. They had to get caught.

Because he seemed anxious that night and couldn't sleep, I fixed my dear husband a nice cup of chamomile tea mixed with pre-workout. Needless to say, sleep had left the building. Not only was he exhausted and couldn't sleep, he was also anxious and restless. Being the great wife I was, I stayed up all night to make sure he was okay. By okay, I mean to make sure he was suffering and indeed he was. I couldn't have been happier.

While caring for my ailing husband, I received a text message from Pamela.

> Pamela: Bitch, here is this mans number. 555-489-8382 and don't ask me for shit else.

> Me: Thank youuuuu. I love you, bestie, and I won't ask you for anything else until the next time I need something lol. Kisses and good night.

> Pamela: Good night, psycho.

I immediately stored the number in my phone and went out back on the veranda to place the call. He didn't answer, so I left a voicemail asking him to get back to me as soon as possible.

The next morning, I made sure to give Jhovan two doughnuts and made him an iced coffee with weight gain powder and progesterone, then sent him off to work tired and sleepy with faulty bid numbers and the wrong address to the bid site. Life was good.

While strategically placing thumbtacks under the rug on his side of the bed, my phone rang, showing Officer Williams's number. I almost broke my neck getting to the phone and sliding accept.

"Hello."

"Well, hello there, Mrs. Stone. How are you?"

"I'm great, now that you've called. And what about you? How are you?"

"I'm good," he muttered. "What can I do for you?"

"Stop being so formal. I hadn't seen you around in a while, and I wanted to check in with you to see how you were doing. I also wanted to thank you for taking care of that ticket for me. That was so kind of you."

"Trust me, not seeing me around is a good thing, and don't bother thanking me. It was the least I could do. You were in a pretty bad way when I gave you that ticket, and if I'm being honest, I felt guilty."

"Why? None of it was your fault. You were just doing your job, and I totally respect that."

"Yes, but it breaks my heart to see a beautiful woman cry. Especially if she's crying due to someone else's wrongdoing."

"Well, we don't have to worry about that anymore. He's old news."

"So you left him? Good for you, Mrs. Stone. I can't tell you how man—"

"Wait, wait, wait. I don't want to lie to you, but I also don't feel the need to tell you my life story either. I have not divorced him...yet. Nor have I moved out...yet. Nor have I broken up with him—"

"Let me guess. Yet," he chuckled.

"Right. Yet. But I'm working on all the above. Things like this take time."

"Yes, things like that can take time. Listen, Mrs. Stone—"

I interrupted with, "Please call me Zaya."

"Zaya, you are a beautiful woman, and I would love nothing more than to spend time with you and get to know you, but I don't date married women or women that are still attached. It comes with too many issues, and I've got enough on my plate as it is."

"I understand. Yes, I'm still married on paper, but trust me when I say to you, my marriage is over. Done. Finito."

"I get it, Zaya, but I don't lik—"

"I come in peace. I'm not trying to stir up any trouble. I just would like to go out for coffee, that's all," I said, cutting him off mid-sentence. "You have been so kind to me. So sweet. Please let me return the favor and at least buy you coffee. We don't have to go anywhere together if it makes you uncomfortable. I could get it and bring it to you. Just tell me where and I'm there."

He quietly spoke, "Are you sure about that, Zaya? Is coffee all you are truly after?"

"I resent that. What makes you think that I need or want anything else from you? I'm simply trying to show you my gratitude. No ulterior motives are present, Mr. Williams. Wait...what's your first name?"

"It's Koda."

"Oh, that's different. Does it have a meaning?"

"Honestly, I've never thought to look it up. I need to do that," he mumbled.

"Yeah, you do. But back to the question at hand. Is coffee cool for you?" I asked as I plopped on my bed and swung my feet in excitement.

"I guess one cup couldn't hurt. I tell you what. My lunch is at 2:00. There's a little shop on the outskirts of town that I frequent often named, *The Mean Bean.* You can meet me there."

My insides gleamed with excitement. "2:00 it is, and I'll see you soon." I hung up smiling at the thought of seeing his handsome face again. I wasn't buying the not-interested bit. His eyes told a different story. I knew that he was trying to be respectful, but there was only one of us concerned about my marriage and it wasn't me. My situation was indeed complicated, so I wouldn't push the issue with Koda. I would just let nature take its course. It always did.

While napping and waiting for 2:00 to hit, my phone buzzed, showing a number I hadn't seen in a while, Sylvia's number. I stared at the phone in disbelief because I knew damn well that two-faced bitch had nothing to say to me. I rolled over and went back to sleep. She called again, and this time I answered.

"Hello."

"Zaya, hi, this is Sylvia. I was taking a chance on calling because I didn't know if you had the same number, but I'm glad to reach you."

"Uh-huh, you got me. What do you want?" I snapped.

"I wanted to reach out to you because India told me that she offered you a position, and I wanted to touch bases with you to make sure that we are good. Well... umm... I know that we aren't exactly good, but I did want to make sure that we don't create a toxic work environment."

I paused, letting what she said sink in.

"Wait, I thought you didn't work there anymore. From what I knew, you bounced a while ago."

"This is true... I did. But once I got my divorce, I moved back to the area and asked for my job back. India was kind enough to let me return. I've been back for six years now, and I don't want any problems between you and me."

"Problems? Oh, you don't have to worry about that. I've mastered the art of ignoring muthafuckas that don't exist in my world. You are one of those people, so I'm cool if you are."

"Zaya, we don't have to do this. We were once very good friends, and if I'm being honest with you, I don't even remember what we were at odds about."

"So you don't remember what we are at odds about, but you remembered that I don't fuck with you? You remembered enough to call me and ask if we are good. Sylvia, you can miss me with the bullshit. You know exactly what you did, and if you don't, I'm sure not going to waste my time reminding you. Have a good day, and don't worry. I won't burst your shit to the white meat like I promised to do the last time I spoke with you. I've grown, and I've got far too much shit going on to worry about your ass. Goodbye."

I hung up, and she called right back.

"Wait... Zaya... please don't hang up. There is something I think you should know."

"And what exactly is that?" I griped.

"Ummm, so, a friend and I went to dinner last weekend, and I saw your husband there with someone else. I wasn't sure if that was him because he looks so different, so I snapped a picture so I could examine it closer. Sure enough, there was that mole perched up on his cheek."

The phone went silent. Only breathing could be heard between the two of us. Breaking the silence, I spoke first.

"So."

"So, is that all you have to say? Are you and Jhovan still married?"

"We are. Like I said, so."

"Oh, okay then. Well, I guess if you don't care, then neither do I. Just in case you're interested, I sent the picture to your phone. It should be coming through in just a minute." I could hear the smile in her voice.

This messy-ass bitch.

"I'm not interested, and it will be deleted the moment it comes through. I'm not even going to open it, but thank you, Sylvia, for your concern. Like I said before, have a good day."

The time to meet Koda was winding down, so I bathed and sauntered to the closet to find something modestly sexy to put on. He'd only seen me looking ragged, and I wanted to wow him a bit without looking like I was trying too hard. I lightly beat my face, curled my long tresses, threw on a cute little romper, heels, and drowned myself in Tom Ford's *Lost Cherry*.

While getting ready, I nearly had a heart attack when I heard the front door slam, followed by footsteps ascending the stairs.

Jhovan stormed into the room, throwing his laptop and briefcase on the bed.

"Hey baby, how are you?" he asked begrudgingly.

"Shit, I'm good. The way you stormed in here, I should be asking you the same thing." Smiling, I shifted my stance away, secretly thrilled because the shit was already hitting the fan.

"This day has been pure hell, Zaya. You know I had a bid to run in Freeport, right?"

"Yes, what about it?"

"The good news is, I won the bid. The bad news is, I somehow beat myself down to my damn socks. I came in about $46,000 cheaper than everyone else. I can't take those kinds of hits. Now we have to practically do this job for damn near free. I won't make a fucking penny on this one," he yelled.

"Oh nooo, babe. How could that have happened?" I smirked as he held his head down.

"The fuck if I know. I know that we are fucked right

now. I've been trying to call Jaime all damn morning, and he's not answering the phone. I sent the numbers to him a few days ago to have him go over them, and he said everything checked out. If they checked out, then how in the fuck could this have happened?" He stood up, unloosened his tie, and unbuttoned his shirt out of frustration.

"First, calm down. I'm sure there is a reasonable explanation for this," I offered.

"Fuck an explanation. I'm trying to figure out how we are going to do this project without faltering on the damn contract. We can't afford to do this shit for practically free. Then, if we try to back out, they could sue us for everything we have. I could lose my company." He sat there with his head in his hands. I put on the saddest face I could muster and rubbed his back.

"It's going to be alright, babe. You're a smart man. You've figured out a solution to every problem you've come across. This is no different. Let me go make you a drink. Maybe that's what you need to calm your nerves," I quipped as I walked toward the bedroom door.

"Thanks, babe," he raised his head. "Zaya, what are you all dressed up for? Looking all good and shit. Where are you going?"

"Oh, I've got a few errands to run before I go get the kids. You know what they say...when you look good, you feel good. I've been feeling a little down about myself lately. I needed a quick pick-me-up, and this did the trick. Anyway, I'll be right back."

I noticed the peculiar look on his face, but I didn't feed into it. Instead, I sauntered down to the kitchen to make his drink. He loved Hennessy, and it was so strong, it masked the flavor of anything mixed with it. It was the perfect drink to doctor up. I sprinkled a little more progesterone along with a dash of laxative powder and took it to him.

While handing him the drink, I added, "Why don't you go take a hot shower and wash your body from head to toe? That always made you feel better. I just changed the sheets. It's nothing like a clean body and fresh sheets."

"I think I will do that. Thanks, babe."

"Anytime. Ummm. I know that you're feeling down and out right now, and I hate to leave you like this, but I've got a couple of meetings to attend. I'll be back in a little bit. Bye." I kissed him on the cheek and headed back out the door. He stood up, wanting to argue. I could tell from the look he gave me, but he wouldn't get the chance. I was out the door before he could utter another word.

CHAPTER 9

Oh, It's Nothing

Putting the name of the coffee shop into the GPS, I quickly backed out the driveway. I waved at Jhovan as he peered from our bedroom window. I smacked my lips and turned my stereo to the max, singing "Lucky Daye" at the top of my lungs:

♪♫ "I don't care 'bout who's around, I just wanna lay you down, I just want you here right now, I just wanna lay you down, and hear you make that fucking sound." ♪♫

Bopping my head and snapping my fingers, I arrived at the location fifteen minutes early. That gave me time to practice what I was going to say to Koda and brush up on my seductress skills. It had been a minute since I felt the need to woo a man. I wasn't sure how this would go, but I was positive my efforts wouldn't be in vain. After all, he was still a man, and I was a beautiful woman with sex appeal.

While talking to myself, I saw his cruiser pull into the front parking space. He slid out of his car, looking like sex on two legs, and jogged over to my SUV. He opened the door and reached for my hand.

"I see you are a punctual person. I like that, Zaya," he offered as we walked side by side into the coffee shop.

After taking a seat, the waitress shot her eyes our way and hurried to our table.

"Good afternoon, Officer Williams," she blushed. "I see you brought company today. That's rare for a busy man like yourself." She looked at me and rolled her eyes. "Should I bring you your regular?" She flashed a smile his way while chewing the end of her pencil.

"No, he doesn't want that today. We are trying something different. Please bring us two medium iced caramel Frappuccinos along with two sandwiches of the day and an extra one for him to take, please. Thank you kindly," I said as I turned my attention back to him.

He chuckled. "Well, just take your dick out and piss all over the table, why don't you."

"What do you mean? Hell, she started it. Listen, I know you aren't my man, but I don't appreciate any woman trying me. Especially these days. It would be nothing for me to rock a bitch's shit, then turn around and let you handcuff me."

"There isn't a need for all that. She's just doing her job. She doesn't mean any harm."

"Shit, tell her that, because she's the one that doesn't know. I'm just here trying to enjoy a nice coffee with a new friend of mine."

"Oh, so we are friends now?"

"So, you aren't my friend, Officer Williams? I think you are. Besides, your name literally means companion/friend. I don't think there's a clearer sign."

"Is that so? I see you took the time to look it up. Woman, you sure are nosy."

"I sure am. I think your name is beautiful. I can tell you what else I discovered about the history of your name, but I'll save that for another time. So, Koda, how has your shift been today? How many crying women's days have you ruined?" I watched the corners of his mouth curl. Dammit, he was beautiful.

"My shift has been good so far, and I haven't ruined anyone's day that I know of. Girl, you've got to let that ticket shit go. I took care of that, remember? What more do you want from me?"

"Don't ask me that. I'd be ashamed to tell you." I winked, and he blushed.

"Here are your drinks and your club sandwiches on

rye. Will you have anything else, Officer Williams, or should I just ask her?" She shot a nasty look my way.

"Girl, if you don't get your bad wig weari—"

"No, thank you, Sasha. That will be all. Thank you so much," he muttered, cutting me off before I could get started. He was laughing so hard, tears were rolling out his eyes. "Damn, you are quick as hell. I need for you to relax, Zaya. Don't let people get to you so easily."

"I normally don't, but damn. I can only take so much. All that shit she's doing isn't necessary, cutting into my time with her foolishness. I'm trying to enjoy my new friend, and it seems like she's hellbent on making that impossible."

"Naw, it shouldn't be that easy for someone to steal that smile off your face. You've got to learn to use your invisible block button. We all have one. Most just refuse to put it to use," he said as he took a bite of his sandwich.

"Or...hear me out...God finally took mine away. He took it away so I couldn't block things that would keep me in the dark. He needed my eyes open, and trust me...they are wide as hell now."

"I'm so sorry. That man hurt the hell out of you, didn't he?" His tone was low now, but serious.

"He did, but I don't want to talk about him."

"Understood. Not another word about him. What do you want to talk about then?"

"I want to know about Koda. Where are you from? What do you do for fun? Do you have any siblings? Are you close with your mother? Why aren't you married? Things like that."

"Oh, so you are really trying to get to know me. And here I was, thinking you just wanted to get in my pants," he laughed.

"I told you I have no ulterior motives. I just want to be your friend, if you would allow it."

"I'm kidding with you, Zaya. Let me see," he raised his finger to his head. "I'm from Tallahassee, and I've been here for nine years now. I have a sister. She's happily married with four kids. My mother passed away when I was nine, but my father is a constant in my life. My old man still resides there, but lately, he's been experiencing signs of early dementia, so he may be coming to live with me soon. The marriage question is simple. I haven't found the right one yet. These days, everyone is into playing games and wants a sponsor. I'm not with any of that shit. Now that you know a little about me, tell me some things about you, Mrs. Stone."

"What would you like to know that you already don't?"

"I only know just a little. I know that you have a husband that isn't your favorite person right now. I also know that you have kids." I side-eyed him because I'd never mentioned my kids. "I saw the booster seats in your SUV. Hmmm...Let's see...what else...Oh, you live in a beautiful exclusive neighborhood, and your husband is in the construction business." I side-eyed him again, but he continued. "I saw the work truck. I also know that you're beautiful even when you cry and your face is smeared with blood, and I also know that you make jokes when you're uncomfortable," he smirked as he raised his glass to his mouth.

"I guess you do know quite a bit. There's not much to tell. Yes, I have children, three of them and I love them more than life itself. I've been married for 14 years, miserably married for seven. I'm from Florala, Alabama, and I came to this city after I graduated college. I came for work but stayed for love. If I knew then what I know now, I would have been on the next thing smoking."

The waitress sauntered back to the table with the check and tried to place it in his hand. I took it from her before she could.

"Umm, thank you, but this lunch is on me. I always keep my promises," I said to him.

"Well, ma'am, I guess that's a nice sentiment, but he eats for free. I'll gladly take your money to pay your half of the tab."

He raised his brow at her, then at me, before looking

down at his phone. I pulled out my card and handed it to her. She walked away without saying a word.

"We will never come back here again. I'm trying to stay out of jail, and women like that trigger the hell out of me. Like seriously, she doesn't know if we are dating or not, but it is clear as day that she doesn't appreciate seeing you with another woman. As a matter of fact, every woman in here has had their eyes on you since we've walked through the door. I mean, you are fine as hell, but damn. They need to learn some decorum...some manners."

He chuckled again. "Thank you so much for the compliment, and these women in here are not studying me."

"Whatever you say. Tell that to their yoking necks and bulging eyeballs." I sneered.

"Well lovely, I would like to thank you for the lunch and the coffee, but duty calls."

"Don't thank me, thank them. I was just company. I told you I wanted to treat you. I didn't treat anyone but myself. So, we've got to do this again—elsewhere," I said, looking around at all the eyes on us.

"I didn't want you spending your money on me. That is part of the reason why we came here."

"Yeah, and you aren't playing fair, but it's okay...I've got your number, and I will use it again. Thank you for meeting with me. I really enjoyed this, and seriously, if it's okay, I would like to do it again."

"I don't think that would be a problem. After work most days, I'm free as a bird. Can you say the same?"

"Koda, if you are asking me if I have to check in or out...the answer is no, but since you've got to run, we can discuss another meet-up later." I smiled at him as he stood and opened his arms for a hug.

I sprung to my feet so quickly, I saw stars. Just as I wrapped my arms around his muscular, sturdy back, the waitress walked up and placed my card, his takeout sand-wich, along with my receipt on the table.

"See you soon, Koda," the waitress said before she walked away.

Still in his arms, I turned to her and said, "You need to work on that nasty attitude of yours. That's why you only got a 5% tip."

He chuckled before releasing me. I didn't want him to let me go. His arms felt like heaven, and he smelled so good.

"So, where are you off to now, Zaya?"

"It's almost three. I have to go pick up my crotch goblins and do a little grocery shopping before heading to the house."

"Don't you mean home?"

"Nope. It doesn't feel much like home anymore. More

like a holding cell until I can get my ducks in a row to leave him," I said as he walked me to my SUV. He grabbed the handle and opened the door for me.

"Well, God doesn't put more on us than we can handle. With that thought in mind, I want you to drive safely, and I will see you around."

"I'll try," I murmured, watching him strut back to his cruiser. Everything about this man was smooth...effortlessly smooth. I'd always been a sucker for a man in a uniform, and he was wearing it like a sin. Koda lit something inside me. My body was awake...aware. By the time I started the car, my thighs were clenched, and my thoughts were straight filthy. My pussy was literally slobbering.

The shit I was going through with Jhovan had nearly killed my libido. But now, it was thumping like a rabbit. Jhovan hadn't stirred me like that in years. That's when it dawned on me: I still wanted connection, passion, and intimacy. I just didn't want it with my husband.

My phone rang. Jhovan's name flashed across the screen. I looked at it once, then dropped it back into the console. Whatever he needed could wait. I was too busy thinking about Koda—the curve of his lips when he smiles, how his arms felt, how his voice wrapped around me. Most of all, I wondered what it would sound like if I made him lose his composure.

After gathering myself, I headed back toward town en

NO LONGER YOURS

route to pick up my children. I arrived at the school just in time to see the second wave of children being escorted to their cars. As I sat there patiently, Ms. Fortress, the teacher's assistant, tapped my window.

Rolling the window down, I muttered, "I see all the other kids coming out, but I don't see my three. Would you happen to know where they are?"

Confused, she clasped her hands together before speaking. "I'm sorry. Mr. Stone came and picked them up already. He was so kind. The kids were surprised but super excited when he arrived. Tell him he should come pick them up more often. It seemed to really make their day."

Forcing a smile, I said, "I'm sure they were excited. Thank you for your help, Ms. Fortress. I will see you later."

I pulled off and placed a call to Jhovan. With a snooty tone, he answered. "So, you finally found the time to call your husband back?"

My mind told me to let him have it, but I had to remember that he didn't know we were beefing. So, I kept my response short and cute.

"Oh, hey baby. I'm sorry. I was in the store when you called the first time. I was going to call you back after I got the kids, but it seems you beat me to it. What's the special occasion?"

"No special occasion, Zaya. Is it so wrong for a husband to pick up his kids?"

❧ 105 ❧

"Not at all. I wish you did it more often. Ms. Fortress told me how excited they were."

"Yes, they were. But seriously, I thought about what you said a while back about how I never took them or picked them up from school, so I wouldn't understand the excitement you got from it. Well, I totally get it now, babe. They made me feel like I was ten feet tall."

Yeah, bitch, but if I could, I'd cut you too short to shit.

Quieting the thoughts swirling in my head, I cleared my throat. "Jhovan, I'm so glad you got to finally experience that. Hopefully that feeling will prompt you to do it more often. Especially since I'm about to start working again, and I'm not sure of the schedule as of yet."

He didn't respond to that statement. Completely ignoring it, he said, "We are going to drive across town and visit my mother. Did you want to come?"

"Hell nawl... I mean, no. I'm good. Are you all going to eat dinner there, or shall I have something ready by the time you get home?"

"I think she's going to cook. She said she had something for me and wanted me to come by. Since I picked the kids up, I figured I would take them with me. You know she loves to see her grandkids."

"Yeah, but that is all she does. Sees them. She hasn't done shit for them since they've breathed air for the first time. She doesn't spend any quality time with them, doesn't call them on their birthdays, she's never even bought a Christmas gift. You know, I find that funny because she always seems to find the time to connect when she needs something. Like that tacky dining room set you got for her last year or that fake Chanel bag she's always carrying."

"Now come on, Zaya. Stop talking about and judging my mama. She does the best she can." His voice was now sharp, annoyed.

"If you say so, but I wasn't talking about her. I was just telling the truth. Why do you get so pissed when I speak on her? You can say what you want about my mother. As long as it's the truth and respectful, I won't argue. Guess we were just raised differently. Anyway, since you all will be out for the evening, I think I'll go grab a burger or something and relax. Tell my babies I love them, and I will see you all when you get home."

"Yeah, whatever. Bye."

I knew he was pissed, but I had always been told it's better to be pissed off than pissed on. He may have thought I was crossing the line a little by coming for his mama, but she was part of the problem. She found nothing wrong with the trifling shit he did and vice versa. She could watch him commit murder in front of her and she would turn her back and say she didn't see him do it. She never corrected him when he did something wrong.

Never!! Instead, she'd make excuses for him and act like it never happened or insinuate that I was being overly sensitive...much like his ass.

Jhovan never wanted to tell or hear the truth if it made him or his family look bad. My thought was, if he was so embarrassed of his truth, then it was up to him to change it. He need not worry, though. I was going to assist him. His whole life was about to change, and it was coming sooner than he knew.

CHAPTER 10

Don't Tell

A little time passed, and as difficult as it was, I kept a poker face while navigating this farce of a marriage. Each day felt heavier than the last. Misery had taken up residence in our home, feeding on both of us but for different reasons.

Jhovan was unraveling, a shadow of his former self. Before his undoing, he had been arrogant, pompous, selfish, and so damn sure of himself it made me sick. But now? He could no longer recognize the man in the mirror. He was losing his sex appeal second by second, and he hated himself for it. For the first time in years...he wasn't HIM. His muscles, once his pride, sagged into soft flesh. Those big guns he previously showed off at every chance were now flabby. His chest was growing, not from strength, but fat, and his belly joined the rebellion. No matter how much he worked out, the scale laughed at him. Hell, his nipples were almost as big as mine. On top of that, he was an emotional, balding mess. A walking midlife crisis in his thirties.

He'd fallen into every trap I'd set for him. Each one tightening the noose I'd crafted out of deceit and patience. He was quickly coming undone...but the truth was, so was I. Playing nice and pretending to care was harder than I thought. It drained me. It was difficult just to be kind. He didn't deserve kindness. What he deserved was to choke on his own lies, to eat shit and wash it down with sewer water. I hated him, down to his bones, and everything he stood for. Jhovan and his actions had unknowingly sucked every ounce of love, patience, and trust I possessed. By this point, I no longer wanted *revenge*. I just wanted *out*.

I found it almost impossible to stroke his ego or play nice. It took too much effort, so I stopped pretending, and silence became my weapon of choice. Most of the time, I ignored him—and it was only then that he felt the shift. I hadn't sucked or fucked him in ages and would cringe when he touched me. When he asked why, I would simply say, "I'm not in the mood."

And I wasn't lying. He didn't do it for me anymore. It had nothing to do with the weight he was putting on or his hairy saucer nipples. It wasn't even the patchy beard or receding hairline. None of that would have mattered if he were the man he pretended to be when we got married. If I were still in love with him, I could love him through anything. His outer appearance wouldn't have phased me. I saw past it when I first met him, but I couldn't see through it now—not with all he'd done. Every time I looked at him, all I saw was rot. He disgusted me.

A month later, I received a call from India letting me know the renovations were complete. I started working the next week. Freedom. Finally, something of my own. I couldn't have been happier. Jhovan tried to act happy for me, but it was written all over his face—he wasn't. He'd lost control, and he could feel it. He complained that work was pulling me away, that the distance between us was growing. He wasn't wrong. But the job wasn't the problem. *I* was.

I was over worrying about his fragile feelings. I'd done enough of that over the years. My plan was simple: work hard, get my name back out there, save as much money as I could, and move forward without Jhovan.

I was putting that plan in motion. I also kept Koda close, talking to him as often as possible, even carving out a few coffee and lunch dates between the madness. He was becoming a constant calm in the middle of my storm. He was peace, and I wasn't letting peace go for anyone.

Only two months had passed since I found those messages in his phone, but time lagged like it had been two years. The tension in the house was suffocating. Then, one night, everything changed. Wanting out was no longer just a want—it was a necessity.

Jhovan was sound asleep beside me when his phone dinged back-to-back. I tried to ignore it, but the rapid succession piqued my interest. I quietly sashayed to his side of the bed to see *Canada Wet* lighting up the screen. My blood turned to lava.

I tiptoed to the veranda and messaged her back.

> Me: She's asleep. Call me.

> Canada Wet: Are you sure?

> Me: Yes. Now, before she wakes up.

Within seconds, the phone rang. I answered but said nothing, letting her speak first. I needed to hear her voice.

"Baby," she breathed heavily, soft and sweet. "I'm tired of this. When are you going to move out? It's been almost a year now. You said you were leaving her but—"

I cut her off. "Don't worry, sweetheart. You'll be getting him soon. He is all yours. I'll even pack his shit for him and have it mailed to your house."

There was a brief silence. "Oh, umm...ummm..."

"No need to stutter, honey. It's okay. Trust me. You don't have to go all silent on me. I've known about you for quite some time now. You're the woman bold enough to send her panties to my house, right? The least you can do is use your words."

"I...I... Look, I shouldn't have done that. It was just... when we first started, I had no idea he was married. He lied to me... and to our girlfriend."

My heart slammed against my chest. "Girlfriend?" I muttered sharply. "What the fuck do you mean 'our girlfriend'?"

"I thought you'd done your research, Zaya. Yes, *our* girlfriend. Jhovan, Calliope, and I... we're in a poly relationship. Jhovan and I were together first, then shortly after, we brought her in. We've been a happy throuple ever since."

I laughed, loud and hollow. "Oh, wow. So, Cauliflower isn't just a side chick to me...she's a side to you as well. Well, ain't that some shit. I... I didn't know that, but it doesn't surprise me. These days, nothing about my husband does. If he's willing to sniff a bitch's dirty panties, lick my ass sweat, and guzzle pussy juice... he'll do anything. As I said, he is all yours. Well, yours and Catnip, or whatever the fuck her name is. I just need one favor."

"What's that?" she whispered.

"Don't tell him we spoke. If you do, he'll try to make things right with me. I don't want to fix it. I want out. I just need a little time and my children and I will be gone. You and Carousel, or whatever the fuck her name is, can have him and this house. I don't want any part of it. I don't want him to do anything but pay child support. I won't even ask for alimony or spousal support because I can support myself. Y'all can have it all."

"So let me get this straight. You're telling me... the mistress, that you don't want him and I can have him? That is crazy, but fine by me. I'll gladly take Big Daddy. He's a good man and a good provider. I got fired from my job, and he pays most of my bills. I'm almost positive he's paying all yours. Why are you so willing to give your husband away? Why give that up?"

I smiled, cold. "Because none of that shit matters to me. I can make my own money, get my own house. What I wanted was loyalty. A faithful, caring husband—a father my children could be proud of. Someone I could trust and depend on. He isn't any of that. Therefore, I. Don't. Want. His. Ass."

"Shit, times are hard out here," she quipped. "You're seriously going to leave a rich nigga in this economy? That is so crazy to me. Damn. Is he that bad?"

"Apparently not to you," I said matter-of-factly. "You're fine with being second, not knowing who he's sleeping with. Fine with the possibility of him bringing home something you can't cure. Fine with sharing him with other women. I could never. I have a healthy pH balance and I would like to keep it that way. Anyhow, are you going to keep this between us or not?"

"I will," she said softly. "And...I know you won't believe me, but...I'm sorry."

"You and you're fucked up pH balance can keep your apology."

I drew in a sharp breath and hung up. She had no idea I was recording our call. I forwarded the recording to my phone, deleted every trace from his, and erased her number from the call log, along with the text messages. Then I slid his phone back onto the nightstand, crawled into bed, and stared into the dark.

The war was far from over. But tonight, I won the battle.

The weekend approached quickly. I decided to take the children to my mother's house for the night. I told Jhovan we'd be back Sunday. He thought it was a friendly family visit, but it was strategy. I needed time and distance to get my shit together.

Once my babies and I arrived, my mother and I got to work. Things at work were going extremely well—better than well. I was making real money for the first time in a long time. According to my calculations, six paychecks would cover rent, deposit, and utilities for a new place. My mother suggested putting everything in her name, just in case.

She and my stepfather offered to help wherever and however they could. Our biggest concern were the kids and how they'd handle me leaving their father. They were young, still resilient, still innocent. I wasn't going to poison that. Whatever happened between us, he'd always be their father. Once the divorce began, so would their counseling.

While we were gone, he called over thirty times. It was like he could feel the shift, smell it in the air. I just prayed Miss Wet kept her word. I wouldn't know for certain until I was face to face with him. He wasn't as good as I was at disguising anger.

We arrived back home midday Sunday, and shit started to hit the fan. I wasn't in the door five minutes before he started in.

"Zaya, why is it that when you are away from me, I can never get you to answer the phone? What's so important that you can't talk to your husband? I feel like I'm always begging you to communicate with me, and I am getting sick and tired of that shit," he scolded.

I tried to hold my tongue, but I couldn't anymore.

I scoffed. "You have the audacity to tell me the shit you're tired of? Let me tell you what I'm tired of. I'm tired of walking into this muthafucka day after day pretending like I want to be here. I'm tired of rolling over to your face every night when what I really want to do is slap it until it turns black and blue. I'm tired of not being able to give my body freely to you without wondering what hole you just crawled out of or whose ass you just ate. I am simply... tired."

"Who do you think you are talking to?" he barked. "Did you forget I'm your husband and not one of your little cronies at work? Nor am I one of the children. You're supposed to respect me."

I let out a bitter laugh. "I'll start respecting you when you start respecting your muthafuckin self. Now stop talking to me, Jhovan. I just got home. I want to get my children situated, relax, and get ready for work tomorrow. The last thing I want is to argue about nothing."

"I'm not trying to argue," he said, voice rising. "I'm just trying to understand. What did I do to make you treat me like I'm invisible? We went to counseling. I thought she was helping you get over the shit from the past. It obviously didn't work. Your attitude is nastier than ever. I don't know how much longer I can take it."

"You don't have to," I said calmly. "Nor do you have to be with me. If you want to leave, just go. I won't stop you. Hell, I might throw a party and put a banner in the sky."

"See? That's the shit I'm talking about. Why do you have to be so damn mean? You act like you hate me."

"I do." My voice cracked with fury. "I do hate you. I hate your ass and everything about you. There, I said it.

Why don't you just leave? Go out there and be who you want to be and stop lying to yourself, because you're not lying to me. You may have fooled your mama and your other family members, but I know exactly who the fuck you are."

"I'm not going anywhere," he said, stepping closer. "And neither are you. We're in this for life. That is just like a woman to want to leave at the first sign of trouble."

The first sign! My blood boiled.

I wanted to scream, to fight, to throw something, to tell him I knew every dirty little secret, every lie, every stain he tried to hide. But I couldn't. Not yet.

I'd planned my exit too carefully to lose control now. He kept picking, and I knew if I didn't get away, I would do something I could not take back.

Instead, I went into the bathroom, shut the door, and breathed. Deep. Slow. Over and over until the fire dimmed. I stayed there what seemed like forever. The house grew quiet. By the time I emerged, he was sprawled across the bed, asleep.

I just stood there, tears sliding down my face.

Because I knew, deep down, this divorce was going to be the fight of my life.

CHAPTER 11

Peace That Passes All Understanding

The moment my eyelids flipped open the next morning, I went out onto the veranda and started making phone calls. First, Pamela... to fill her in and tell her to be on standby, just in case I needed her. Then, I dialed Koda.

"Hey, Shug. How are you this morning?" I asked.

"I can't complain. What's going on with you? You've been missing in action for a few days."

I exhaled sharply. "A lot. You sure you want to hear the fuckery that is my life?"

"Of course I do. Hit me. I'm off today anyway, I've got time." he replied.

"He's unraveling," I said flatly. "He knows he's lost control, and he's not handling it well. He can feel it. God gave us women's intuition. What did He give y'all?"

Koda chuckled, low and weary. "Zaya, I can't speak for every man, but when the shift in your woman happens, you just know. Why do you say he's unraveling? Did he do something?"

"He didn't *do* anything. It's what he said. We got into it last night. I told him to just leave...to go be who he wanted to be. You know what he said? *'I'm not going anywhere, and neither are you.'*"

"I don't know, Zaya..." he grunted. "That sounds like a threat to me. You need to watch him. He knows you're done, but he doesn't sound like he's accepting it."

"He isn't. And that's what makes me so angry because he doesn't have a choice. He disrespected me, cheated on me for years, paid another woman's bills, in a whole throuple, and now he's pissed because *I* want out? His entitlement should be studied because what in the hell did he think would happen once I found out his ass was still lying like a Persian rug?"

Koda sighed. "Most men carry what my father calls *the man spirit*. It's when you know you're wrong, but pride won't let you admit it. I've seen it destroy good women. The ones who only came to love, to build, to make life better. That spirit will run them off every time."

"Well, the man spirit done possessed him. He's lost touch with reality." I tried to laugh it off. "Anyway, enough about me. Since you're off, what are you doing today?"

"I'm heading out to see my father. Want to come with?"

My voice hitched in my throat. "Are you serious? I don't know if I'm ready to meet Pops. Will he be okay with me coming?"

"My father loves company. All old people do," he chuckled.

Smiling, I announced, "I'm going to see a divorce attorney after I drop the kids off, then I'll be free. So yes, I'd love to ride with you."

"I'm taking the Harley today. You ever been on the back of a motorcycle?"

"No, but there is a first time for everything. I'll call you when I'm done. Where should we meet?"

"I live out in the boonies, surrounded by bushes and sticks. You can leave your car here so nobody sees you or tells him your whereabouts. That okay with you? Do you trust me?"

"Yes, I trust you. You've been nothing but an angel on earth to me. Why wouldn't I?"

I could feel his smile through the phone.

"Alright then. I'll send you the addy shortly. Just come on over after the attorney's office, and we'll head out."

"See you soon," I said softly.

"Zaya!!"

Jhovan's voice thundered through the air, making my

soul almost leap out of my body. "Who are you out here on the phone with?"

I turned, irritated. "What does it matter to you? Go back inside and leave me alone, please."

He stood there, fire burning in his eyes.

"Let me ask you something, Zaya and you better not lie to me. Are you fucking somebody else?"

"Ha." I laughed bitterly. "I'm not fucking anybody. Not even you. Unlike you, I don't go around sharing myself with randoms. And even if I *was*, I'd be well within my rights, don't you think?"

"What the fuck is wrong with you? Why are you acting so stupid?" He questioned and just as he stepped closer, Jr. came out onto the patio.

"Mama, there isn't any music playing or coffee brewing. How are we supposed to get ready without our pregaming music?"

I forced a nervous chuckle. "Mama's sorry, baby. Go on inside. I'll be in there in a minute, okay?"

He rubbed his sleepy eyes and went back in.

I turned back to Jhovan, voice low and steady. "Listen to me and listen well. You don't scare me. So quit running up on me like you're gonna do something. All I asked last night was for you to leave me alone and I'm asking for the same thing today. I am not your daughter, and I don't answer to you. Now, I'm going to get myself and the kids ready. I suggest you do the same."

I brushed past him, refusing to look back.

The rest of the morning hung heavy with silence. The only words I could muster were *goodbye* as the kids and I shuffled to the car.

All I could think about was Koda. His calm energy. His steady presence. The way he didn't have to say much, his silence spoke enough. He wasn't chasing attention, just quietly watching, assessing. There was purpose behind those eyes. And I wanted to know all of it.

This divorce couldn't happen fast enough.

After catching my babies' morning kisses, I called my mother and stepfather. I told them everything...his words, his behavior, my fears. I needed everyone to know, just in case.

"I'm headed to Tallahassee with Koda for a quick trip," I said.

Mama sighed. "Now, I know you and Jhovan are done, but you're still a married woman. Don't open that door with that young man until the other one is closed. Don't mess this up either. He could be your next ex-husband," she giggled.

"Mama, you are wrong for that."

"I'm just playing, baby. But be careful. Make sure he

takes care of you. Tell him you need to come back the same way you left, unhurt and unscathed. If one hair is out of place, your stepfather and I will be on his ass like stank on shit."

"Mama," I chuckled. "All that isn't necessary. He's a whole state trooper. Gentle as summer rain. He's not the one I'm worried about...it's *that husband of mine* that I have to watch."

"Oh, don't worry. I'm calling his ass next. Everybody's getting some straightening today. Especially since his own mama won't do it."

I sighed. "I guess we are all heathens who should be stoned and burned at the stake for our sins."

"That's not what I'm saying, Zaya." Her tone softened. "You've spoiled that man for years, treated him like a king even when he didn't deserve it. He's not going to handle this separation well. Samson and I were talking last night. We think once the papers are filed, and before he gets served, you and the kids should come stay with us. Or move into my old house. You know, the one you grew up in?"

"I appreciate that, but I don't want to move back. I'd have to drive an hour and a half to work every day, and I'm not doing that. Don't worry, Mama. I've got a plan."

"Okay, baby. I'll let you handle it. Just know we're always here."

"I love you, Mama. I'll talk to you later."

Hanging up, I made one last call to India to request the day off. She agreed without hesitation.

I pulled into the attorney's office parking lot and cut the engine.

"Here goes nothing," I whispered, stepping out of my SUV.

The waiting room was bright and smelled of lemon polish and anxiousness. I sat there twiddling my thumbs and clutching my purse like it was the last thing tethering me to my sanity. The longer I sat, the harder my heart thumped.

"Mrs. Stowe?" the receptionist called.

I stood, legs shaky but determined. "It's *Mrs.* Stone, actually," I corrected softly, and followed her down the hall.

The attorney's office was bright, organized, and too calm. A tall woman with box braids, fitted business suit, bangles and sharp eyes stood to greet me. Her nameplate read *Altunia Rotwell, Family Law.*

Warmly, she said. "Please, have a seat. You must be Zaya."

"That's me," I forced a small smile.

"So," she began, opening a manila folder, "tell me what's been going on."

I took a deep breath. "Where do I start? My husband.

He's been cheating for years. I found out about three women, possibly more. Lately, he's become increasingly controlling, manipulative, and I'm done. I can't take him anymore. That's why I'm here."

She nodded slowly, pen gliding across paper. "Do you have evidence of the betrayal?"

"Oh, yes ma'am. I've got plenty. Text messages, call logs, photos, videos, and I even have a recording of one of the women admitting to their affair."

"Good," she said, glancing up. "That's going to help a lot. Do you share any property together? Cars, house, business?"

"All of the above," I said, bitterly. "And he's a contractor. I know the books aren't clean. There's a lot of money floating around that he hasn't reported. I know him, he's going to cry broke. He isn't. I just want my children cared for."

Her brows lifted slightly. "We'll request full financial disclosure. And we'll freeze joint accounts if necessary to keep him from moving money around."

My heart thudded. "Is that... safe to do?"

Altunia leaned forward. "Zaya, I've handled worse. You're not the first woman to sit in that chair afraid of her husband's reaction. But once we file, you'll have legal protection. He can't touch you. Not without consequences."

Something inside me trembled. "That's the part that rattles me most...His reaction. He's already said I'm not going anywhere."

Her gaze softened. "That sounds like intimidation. Do you believe he's capable of hurting you?"

"I don't know," I said softly. "If you'd asked me the same thing last week, I would have said no. But now...I'm not sure. I'm sure he wouldn't hurt our children though."

Altunia sat back, tapping her pen gently. "Alright. We'll make a plan. I'll prepare the petition for divorce, a temporary restraining order if needed, and paperwork for joint custody. You'll have options."

I nodded, relief flooding me so fast it made me nauseous. "Thank you."

"You're doing the right thing," she said. "This is your first step towards your freedom from it all. The lies, the cheating and whatever else that prompted you to begin these proceedings."

Inhaling sharply, I got up and trekked back to my SUV. The air already felt different, lighter but heavy at the same time. My hands shook as I reached for my phone.

I texted Koda and he replied seconds later.

> Me: Just finished. I did it. Paperwork's in motion.

> Koda: Proud of you. I'll be waiting.

By the time I pulled up to Koda's place, my nerves were still dancing from the attorney's office. The conversation had been empowering, but the reality of it all weighed heavy on me. Divorce. That word carried weight. It wasn't just papers and signatures. It was the burial of years, of promises, of the man I thought I was marrying.

KODA'S HOME sat at the end of a long gravel driveway, tucked between pine trees and wildflowers. It wasn't big or fancy, it was *intentional.* Everything about it felt grounded, masculine, and peaceful. Much like him. A wide porch wrapped around the front with two rocking chairs, a swinging bench, and the faint scent of hickory hung in the air. Wind chimes sang softly above the doorway. This was true country living and I was here for it.

I exhaled for what felt like the first time all day.

When Koda stepped out, my heart did that thing again... skipped, then stuttered. This was my first time seeing him out of uniform and dammit he was fine. I didn't think it was possible for him to look better. He had on dark jeans, a fitted tee, and boots, a pair of black gloves tucked into his waistband. The sun caught his smile, and I swear I forgot my name for a second.

"You found me," he said, walking toward me.

"Yeah," I said, half-laughing, half-sighing. "I was about to turn around. I thought maybe my GPS was tripping. You weren't lying when you said you lived in the sticks. Boy, you don't ever have to worry about anyone popping in on you."

He grinned. "It's supposed to feel hidden. Peace doesn't live on main roads."

"Yeah, I can see that," I murmured, glancing around. "It's beautiful out here. Quiet. You built all this by yourself?"

"Every nail and board. I needed a place that couldn't hear the world. Somewhere I could breathe, so I built one."

"Well, you nailed it. Literally." I smiled.

He laughed softly and motioned toward the porch. "Come in for a second before we go. You want water, tea?"

"Water's good," I said, following him up the steps.

Inside, the place was spotless. Not sterile but *curated*. Dark wood floors, high open beams, brown leather couch, plants thriving in the corners. His home smelled of pine and something else familiar...him. It was sturdy and unbothered like it's owner.

"You can sit anywhere you like," he said, handing me a cold bottle. "You look like your brain's running a mile a minute. You want to talk about it?"

I sat, twisting the cap off. "It is."

He tilted his head. "How'd everything go?"

"I signed the paperwork to start the process," I said quietly. "She's filing within forty-eight hours."

He nodded, lips pressing together. "That's big. You okay?"

"I don't know," I admitted. "I thought I'd feel happy right away. But instead, I feel like I just jumped off a building and I'm waiting to hit the ground."

He leaned against the wall with his arms folded. "That's normal. You've been holding everything together for years. The fall feels weird at first, but it's just your soul preparing you for your landing."

I looked at him, studying the calm in his eyes. "You talk like you've done this before."

He smiled faintly. "No, I haven't but I know when someone is tired and searching for relief. I know wanting peace so badly, you could taste it, and I also know peace when I see it. It's sitting right in front of me."

My stomach flipped.

"It's funny how you see peace and all he saw was somebody he could play with. How does that work?"

"I honestly don't know, Zaya. You are a good person. Good intentions. From the beginning, I've gotten nothing but genuine vibes from you. Even seeing you for the first time with tears in your eyes and blood on your shirt. I saw a beautiful woman who was just trying to survive the cards she'd been dealt. Anyhow, let's not get too deep."

He motioned toward the door. "You ready for that ride?"

A nervous laugh escaped me. "As ready as I'll ever be."

CHAPTER 12

Letting Go

O utside, the Harley gleamed like polished midnight. The leather seat caught the sunlight, and my pulse jumped as he handed me a helmet.

"Let me remind you, I've never ridden on one of these. The closest I've gotten is seeing them in the movies. When I was a little girl, I did want to be Appolonia," I giggled.

"Well, I'm no Prince, but I can tell you that you're in for a time," he said with a wink. "Hold on tight and trust me."

And I did. The engine roared to life, low and guttural with a heartbeat of its own. When he told me to get on, I swung a leg over and gripped his waist, and my stomach began doing backflips... my pussy too.

We took off down the winding road, the trees blurring

into green streaks. The air hit my face, sharp and clean, and I couldn't stop smiling.

Every mile put more distance between me and the chaos I'd been dealing with. I wasn't thinking about being watched, judged, or needed. I was just being.

Wind whipped through my hair and stung my cheeks, but I didn't care. I clung to him, not out of fear, but out of something steadier... trust. Every lean, every turn, every shift of his body told me he knew exactly where he was going, and somehow that steadied me too.

The road opened wide as we crossed into Tallahassee. Moss hung low from ancient oak trees. Then he finally turned onto a narrow dirt road with old fence posts and tall grass, my heart raced again.

"Where are we?" I asked, shouting over the engine.

"My father's place," he yelled back. "You'll see."

We rolled to a stop in front of a small white house with chipped paint and a wraparound porch that had clearly seen better days. A garden bloomed on one side, collard greens, okra, tomatoes, squash—all growing and thriving. An old cowbell hung from the door.

Koda cut the engine, and the sudden silence felt thick, sacred almost. I removed my helmet and blinked, taking it all in.

"This is beautiful," I said quietly.

He smiled faintly. "He built it himself when I was

little. He swore this land would always be ours. Guess I took after him more than I realized."

The screen door creaked open, and an older man stepped out, leaning slightly on a cane. His face lit up the second he saw Koda. "Well, look what the wind blew in!" he called, voice warm but trembling.

Koda grinned wide...an open, boyish grin I hadn't seen before. "Hey, old man," he teased, climbing the steps. "You still remember who I am?"

His father chuckled, eyes sparkling. "Course I do. You're the boy who still owes me twenty bucks from that time you lost at dominoes."

Koda laughed, wrapping him in a hug so tight I had to look away for a second. There was something so tender about that moment. When they finally parted, Koda turned back toward me.

"Pop, this is Zaya. My friend."

His father's eyes found mine, kind and knowing. "Well now, Zaya," he said with a smile. "You're even prettier than your name sounds. You come to make sure my son's behaving himself?"

I laughed softly. "Somebody has to."

"Good," he said. "He was always a handful. Don't let that quiet act fool you. This boy used to be bad as hell when he was younger."

"Alright, alright," Koda said, shaking his head. "You need anything before we sit out back?"

"Just some company," his father replied. "And maybe a glass of that lemonade you make so good."

"Coming right up." Koda disappeared into the kitchen like it was muscle memory.

I followed his father out to the porch. The view was breathtaking. The sunlight spilled across the fields, the beautiful sound of birds singing in the distance. The air was thick with quiet. He sat down slowly, patting the chair beside him.

"My son tells me you've been going through something," he said softly.

My chest tightened. "You could say that."

He nodded. "He didn't tell me what, but whatever it is... just remember, storms don't last forever. They often come, wash away what you shouldn't have been holding onto and go about its business. You're gonna be ok."

Before I could respond, Koda came back with three tall glasses of lemonade. He handed one to his father first, making sure it was within reach, then passed one to me. The small gesture didn't seem like much, but it spoke volumes. The way he watched his father sip carefully, how he adjusted the chair so the sun wasn't in his eyes, how he listened when his father started a story he'd clearly told a hundred times... it was... everything.

Finally, I saw Koda not as the quiet man who had been helping me keep my sanity, but as a caretaker, a son, a protector. A man who loved deeply and without fanfare.

His father started humming an old blues tune, and Koda joined in without missing a beat. Their laughter mixed with the sound of birds singing made my throat tighten. This... this was what safe looked like. It wasn't fancy or loud. It was patient. It was kind.

We sat outside and talked for hours. Koda's father yawned. A soft reminder it was time for his nap. Koda helped him inside, settling him into bed with the kind of gentle assurance that only comes from years of devotion. Watching him, something deep inside quaked. I wasn't just impressed. I was moved.

He came back outside, the afternoon sun glowing across his face. "He likes you," he said simply.

"I like him too," I murmured. "He's... special."

Koda nodded. "Yeah. He doesn't remember much anymore. Some days he thinks I'm his brother. Some days he doesn't know me at all. But when he smiles like that, just for a second, it's like the world stops hurting."

My voice barely came out. "That's love, Koda."

He looked at me, and the air between us shifted again... it was soft, it was... real.

"Yeah," he said quietly. "It is."

I didn't want to leave his father without saying my good-bye, so I quickly walked back in to find him sound asleep. I kissed him on the cheek and exited back out the door.

"Are you ready to ride Mrs. Stone, soon to be Ms. Stone?"

"I sure am," I chirped as I hopped on the Harley.

THE RIDE BACK FELT DIFFERENT. Quieter. I held onto Koda's waist, pressed my cheek against the back of his shoulder and let the rumble of the Harley drown out the noise in my head.

He had one hand on the throttle, the other resting easy, but I could still feel his strength through the small movements. He wasn't just driving the bike, he was owning it. Confident and sure, he didn't have to say anything for me to feel safe. His calm wasn't an act; it was part of him, woven into every word, every breath.

We rode in silence for miles, and I couldn't stop thinking about what I'd seen. How gently he'd wiped the crumbs from his father's shirt, how he'd hummed along to the blues like a man who'd learned patience from pain. How his eyes softened every time his father forgot his name but remembered his heart. Koda was gentle but firm, calm but full of life. There was no resentment in his eyes, only love. And that, more than anything, made me see him differently.

It wasn't just kindness, it was devotion.

And it hit me that I'd never had someone pledge that kind of devotion to me.

Not Jhovan. Not anyone. I was always the one giving the most.

That realization stung, but it also felt like waking up from a long sleep.

Somewhere between the road and the whisper of the wind, I started to cry. Quiet tears that I hoped he wouldn't feel against his back. Not out of sadness, but out of release. I wasn't angry, and I wasn't pretending. I wasn't trying to fix or prove anything. I was just... free.

When we finally pulled back into his driveway, I climbed off the bike and took a deep breath, already missing the breeze across my cheeks.

"You alright?" he asked, pulling off his helmet. His voice was low, careful.

"Yeah," I said, wiping my cheeks quickly. "Just thinking."

He nodded, taking a slow step closer. "About what?"

"About peace," I admitted. "How it feels like something you have to earn, not something that just shows up one day."

He gave a small smile. "You're right. It's like rebuilding a house, piece by piece, quietly, without an audience."

"Your dad," I said softly. "He's... beautiful. The way you care for him, it's rare. Most people run from responsibility. You're running toward it."

Koda looked down for a second before he spoke. "That's the thing about love. You don't get to choose the parts you care for. You have to take it all, the good, the broken, the fading. Especially the fading."

His words hit something deep inside me, like my soul recognized the truth in him.

He studied me for a moment before removing my helmet. "You need a minute before you drive home? I can make us coffee, or you can just sit for a while."

I shook my head, smiling softly. "If I stay, I might not leave."

His eyes lingered on mine. "Then maybe that's not the worst thing."

The air thickened as we gazed at one another. It was gentle but not rushed. There was no seduction in his gaze, just quiet understanding.

"Well, maybe I could stay just a little while longer. I think I'll ask Jhovan to get the kids from school. Give me one minute," I said as I turned my back to place the call.

I dialed Jhovan. It only rang once.

"What, Zaya?!?!" His voice came out sharp, already

irritated. "Now you wanna talk. This morning you didn't want me to say shit to you."

I exhaled slowly. "I still don't, but I need you to pick the kids up for me, please."

"Pick the kids up?" he repeated, his tone dripping with annoyance. "Why can't you do it? Let me guess, you're too busy for your own family."

I clenched my jaw. "Jhovan, I'm not doing this with you. I just need you to get the kids. That's all I'm asking."

"What kind of mother puts other shit before her children? You knew before you took that fucking job what your responsibilities were, but you were so busy trying to get back to work that you didn't consider this type of shit happening. You do realize that most days I'm not in the office, I'm usually on job sites and I don't have time to stop and get the kids," he snapped. "You're too busy out there playing boss lady. Too busy out there pretending I don't exist!" he barked.

Before I could respond, I heard the straw rustling beneath his feet. Koda came and stood right beside me. His eyes were narrowed, his jaw tight. He didn't say a word, but the anger in his expression said enough.

"Are you done? Because who in the fuck are you talking to like that?" I asked Jhovan quietly. "If you're finished insulting me, the kids still need a ride home.

Either you pick them up, or I'll call Mama, but Mama didn't fuck and help make them, you did."

"I'll get them this time, but you're pushing it, Zaya," he said, his voice dropping lower, darker. "Keep acting like this and see where it gets you."

"Goodbye, Jhovan." I hung up before he could finish whatever threat he was building.

The silence after was heavy. I turned to Koda. "I'm sorry you had to hear that. I have a bit of a potty mouth sometimes. Oddly enough, he's the only one that brings that out of me."

Koda stepped closer, his voice low and controlled. "He always talk to you like that? That was a damn threat, Zaya."

I hesitated. "No, but as I told you, he's angry because I won't talk to him. And because he doesn't know my every move."

Koda's nostrils flared. "Nah. That ain't anger. That's disrespect. Don't normalize that shit."

I looked down, my throat tight. "I know. I'm just trying to make it through the process without starting a war."

He shook his head slowly. "You don't have to start one. He already did, and you need to strap up your boots."

The words hit me hard. They were too true to ignore.

Koda walked to the front door, his tone steady but

laced with something protective. "Next time he raises his voice to you, put him on speaker. I want to hear it."

I blinked. "Why?"

"So I can explain to him what a real man sounds like when he talks to a woman."

I didn't know what to say. The mix of calm fury and quiet care in his voice was admirable. He didn't raise his tone. He didn't threaten. But there was a promise in his eyes.

He opened the door for me, his hand brushing mine. "Come on, Zaya. Let's have a nice cup of coffee. You've done big girl things today, and I think you deserve it," he grinned.

I laughed softly despite the heaviness in my chest. "Damage control seems to be my new specialty."

"Good," he said with a small smile. "Because something tells me you're about to need it."

Once inside his house, I took the time to really look around at the family photos on the walls. Faded awards from his service. I ran my fingers across a framed photo of him and his dad. "This is such a nice, cozy place. I wasn't really expecting you to live like this."

He smirked, that deep, unbothered grin tugging at his mouth. "What, you expected chaos?"

"Honestly?" I laughed. "Yeah. Maybe a pizza box or

two, a pile of laundry, a stripper pole. You give bachelor energy."

He chuckled, shaking his head. "Nah. I like things neat and quiet. Too much noise in my line of work. Gotta come home to something that makes sense."

We talked for a while. Nothing forced. Nothing shallow. Just real conversation. I told him about the decline of my marriage and what I'd recently discovered about my husband. He told me about his ex and how she couldn't handle the hours, the distance, the heaviness of his job. He said it without bitterness, just acceptance.

"I used to think if something you wanted so badly to work didn't, it meant you were a failure," he said, staring into his glass. "But it just means it wasn't meant for you, and if you gave it time, something better would come around the corner."

I nodded, my throat tight. "You sound like someone who's been through a lot."

He looked at me then, his gaze quiet. "And you sound like someone who's still in it."

That one line stripped me bare, knocked me clean off my shit.

The distance between us was shifting. I didn't even realize I'd moved closer until I could feel his breath against my skin.

CHAPTER 13

Just Say It

"Koda..."

He reached out, fingers brushing a stray curl from my face. "Zaya..."

My heart was thundering. Every nerve in me wanted to close the distance, but then he pulled back ...slow and deliberate. His jaw flexed.

"I can't," he whispered. "Not like this. Not while you're still his."

The restraint in his tone made my knees weak. I wanted to throw him down and drain him dry. I also wanted to be angry at him for resisting me, but I couldn't. I respected him for it. It turned me on and made me want him even more. My pussy was thumping.

Before I could respond, my phone buzzed on the counter.

Jhovan's face lit up the screen once again.

My stomach dropped. I answered. "Hello?"

"Where the hell are you, Zaya?" His voice was sharp, loud enough that Koda looked up immediately. "After I picked up the kids, I went by your job... they said you took today off. You got me out here lookin' stupid?" He growled.

"I had some things to take care of. I didn't want to argue about it, sort of like you are trying to do now," I said quickly, my voice barely steady.

"Don't lie to me!" he snapped. "Where are you? What nigga you fucking?"

Koda's whole expression changed. His shoulders squared, his eyes darkened. I could feel the tension radiating off him.

"Tell him not to talk to you like that," Koda said quietly, but his tone left no room for argument.

I hesitated. "Jhovan, I'll call you back."

"Zaya...don't you fucking hang up on me!"

I did.

For a second, I couldn't breathe. A golf ball sized lump sat heavy in my throat ...thick enough to choke on.

Koda stepped closer, his voice low. "I told you the next time he talked to you like that to let me talk to him."

Before I could say anything else, my phone buzzed again. It was Pamela's face this time.

I answered, voice trembling. "Hey."

"Girl, what is going on?" Pamela's voice was hushed but panicked. "Jhovan just left here lookin' for you. Said you weren't at work. I didn't know what to say, Zaya. He looked like some kind of fucking mad maniac."

"Are you serious Pamela?"

"Yes, he caught me as I was on my way back to my cruiser. I stopped back by my house to grab something, and he pulled up damn near on two wheels. Your babies were in the backseat. They were smiling and shit so that's a good thing but girl, speaking from a law enforcement perspective, you may need to get a restraining order. I'm telling you. Something is happening with him. His eyes didn't look right, and you know I've seen crazy before."

Goosebumps trailed up my arm. "He came to your house with my babies?"

"Yeah. And he was pacing. You need to be careful, Zay."

"I will," I whispered. "Thanks, Pam."

When I hung up, Koda was standing by the window, fists clenched, chest rising slow and controlled. Anger was etched across his face.

"He went to your friend's house?" His tone was calm, but I could hear the angst sitting just beneath it.

I nodded, my voice small. "Yeah."

He grabbed his jacket off the chair. "He wants to play crazy? I can play crazy too."

I stepped in front of him. "Koda, please. I don't want you involved in this mess. I won't let you risk your safety or your career. He's not worth it."

He looked down at me, then softened. Sighing, he set the jacket back down.

"So, you think it's ok to risk your own life? Zaya...are you not listening? Your friend just told you he didn't look like himself. Let's go get your children now. You all can come back here."

"'Koda, that's a nice sentiment but I refuse to disturb your peace. You deserve it. I have three children, three sweet but rambunctious children. I'm sure you aren't used to the noise and they would all but destroy your house."

"Zaya, what does that have to do with the price of tea in China? I don't care about any of that shit. What I care about is you and those kids being safe. You are more than welcome to stay here if you like. If you don't want to stay here, I will arrange lodging until we can figure something else out. The point is, you don't need to be around someone who's clearly unstable and neither does your children," he expressed.

Lifting my chin, he continued, "You know what I do for work. I've seen things involving kids that brought grown men to their knees. Men use children to get back at their spouses all the time. Don't ever think it can't happen to you, Zaya. I'd rather you be safe than sorry."

"Ok, I'm going to leave and go get them. The thing is, I'm not sure how he's going to react to me taking them."

"And I don't blame you for being concerned about that. That's why I'm going with you," he voiced.

"I don't think that's a good idea, Koda. If he sees you, he is liable to freak out even worse. Just let me go and gauge the temperature first."

"Beg my pardon but that's crazy. I tell you what. I'll trail you and park right up the street. I want you to call me on the phone and put me in your pocket, your purse...wherever you need. I need to hear everything. If he gets crazy, I'll be there in a second. Does that work for you?"

"It does. Thank you for doing this. I know we are just starting to know each other a little better but if this is too much for you, I'd understand if you didn't want to see me anymore after this."

"I'm careful, but I'm not a pussy, Zaya. Let's go," he demanded.

My hands trembled the entire way home. I didn't know what to expect when it came to Jhovan, but I knew it wouldn't be good. He had practically breathed fire through the phone.

Koda trailed behind me in his old school Chevelle and

just as promise, he parked at the house just before mine. Before I hopped out the car, I dialed Koda's phone number and placed the phone in my pocket, microphone facing upwards. Then, I trekked to the front door. I walked into silence, and it made my blood run cold. There was no laughter, bumps, ruckus or sounds coming from any of the children's bedrooms. I searched for them everywhere. There was no sight of them. No book bags either. I ascended the steps to find Jhovan sitting in the mirror staring at himself.

"Jhovan, where are the children? They aren't in their rooms."

He didn't reply. He continued to stare.

"Jhovan, did you hear me? I asked where are my children?" My voice trembled with each word.

"They are at my mother's. I took them and dropped them off because you and I need to talk alone."

"I don't want to talk, Jhovan. I'm done talking to you. My words seemed not to matter to you anymore, so I stopped using them. Now I use my silence."

He shifted in the chair. "Zaya, that wasn't me asking you to talk to me. That was me telling you."

Scoffing, I muttered, "And just like I told you earlier, you are not my father. I don't know where his ass is, but you are not him. I just came to get my children and a couple of clothes. I'm not staying here tonight, and neither are they. You're acting like a lunatic, and you need to cool off so I'm going to give you time to do that."

I trekked towards the walk-in closet to get my suitcase. He stood up and walked towards me. His eyes were dark... cold.

He smirked before he spoke. "I know what you know, Zaya. Now I understand why you've been so pissed at me."

"I don't know what you're talking about, Jhovan. I just want to get what I need and leave." I quipped.

Now standing directly in front of me, he lifted my chin with his finger and asked, "Are you trying to leave me for one night, or for good. Because I heard it was for good." He let out a small chuckle. "That's what you told Solee right? That's what you said wasn't it? You told that bitch she could have me. How in the fuck are you going to give me away to someone? What kind a wife does that?"

"The kind that's tired of you and your shit," I shouted. "Jhovan, if you know what I know, then you understand why I want to get the fuck away from you. You've been in a whole relationship with two other women, doing what you want when you want."

"But what does any of that have to do with us? That doesn't change anything. You are my wife, and I am your husband. What me and those bitches have going on hasn't affected us. "Zaya," his voice thundered. "Husbands and wives don't just leave each other."

"Are you fucking kidding me right now. Yes, they do when your husband has 'peace,' somewhere else. Isn't that what you told her she was...your peace. Go get your peace over there. I sure as hell wish I had somewhere I could go get peace because it's not here. I would be a glutton for punishment to stay in this marriage so to answer your question, yes, I'm leaving you for good, but not at this very moment. Right now, I just want to grab a few things and go somewhere until I can figure this thing out."

Scoffing, he mumbled, "There is nothing to figure out. You are not leaving me and I'm for damn sure not going to let you take my children away from me."

"First off. Stop fronting. You don't give a fuck about the kids. You never have. I believe you loved the idea of them, but that's about it. You don't know my babies for real. You've never taken the time to truly know them. You probably don't even remember their middle names, or their favorite color. I have to remind you every year of their birthdays. Someone who gave a fuck would know.

Second, you need to realize that you don't own me, Jhovan, and you don't have the right to tell me I can't leave you. You pushed me away with all the bullshit you've been doing. Cheating, lying, sniffing other women's nasty ass panties. Was I supposed to stay and let you run over me like some kind of fool? No, not me." I spat.

"I wasn't trying to run over you, Zaya. I was just into some shit I figured you wouldn't understand," he alleged.

"Yeah, and that's a problem. I would have done just about anything for you before all this shit happened. Did you really think I would never find out? Did you? Because I've never been a goofy bitch, Jhovan, and you know this. You're selfish and entitled. You're not sorry for any of the shit you've done. You're sorry you got caught."

"Staying with you is on me though. I should have left you when it happened the first time, but I tried to make it work. I pushed my wants and needs to the side for you, and you cheated again. Hell...you never stopped. And as far as the children, I'm not trying to take them from you. I would never do that. I am trying to keep the peace, and you are making that damn near impossible with the way you've been acting. With all your threats and popping up where you don't belong... I'm not going to stand for that shit. You can't scare me into submission."

"Zaya, I'm not trying to scare you, and you know I would never hurt you. You think you're slick. It's some-body else you're trying to get to, isn't it? That's why you are trying to leave me... Somebody else has got you acting different. Your ass ain't scared of me or what I might do. I've never known you to be scared of anybody, man or woman. You just don't want to be here. Just say it." He scoffed.

"I did say it. I told you last night I didn't want to be here, and I was tired of pretending. You don't listen to me. You never listen to me."

"Tell me...what's with all this, 'You need to calm down shit,' do you really think that I would hurt you girl? I've never laid a finger on you or my children. What makes you think that I would start hurting you now?"

"Maybe the two or three threats that you have issued out and as far as hurting me, you've hurt me mentally already...what's to stop you from hurting me physically?"

He stood there dumfounded. Not knowing where to take the conversation next. He grabbed the back of his neck, then murmured, "Whatever you say, Zaya. If you need a night to think about what you are doing, I'm OK with that. Just know that I expect my kids to be here when I get home from work tomorrow. And I'm not playing with you."

"See, there you go threatening me again. What's gonna happen if they are not here, huh? What are you going to do?"

"Let my children not be here when I get here and you will find out." Flexing his fingers and cracking his knuckles, he muttered, "Go ahead and pack what you need to pack and get the fuck out. I'll call moms and tell her you're coming to get the kids."

Without saying another word, I grabbed my suitcase

from the closet and began stuffing clothes into it. Once I was done in my closet, I went to my children's room, grabbing what I could and bolted out the front door. My heart was beating so heavy in my chest that I got lightheaded. Koda, watching from the distance, saw me struggling with the luggage and bags and ran to help.

By the time he reached me, I was hyperventilating. Peering up at my bedroom window, I could see my husband watching us. With the last bit of breath that I had in my lungs, I attempted to tell Koda he was watching but slipped out of consciousness.

"Zaya!" Koda's voice sounded distant, like it was coming from underwater. I felt weightless, floating in and out of darkness. Then there was the pressure, his strong arms wrapping around me. My body swayed with every step he took.

"Stay with me, Zaya...stay with me," he muttered, his breath trembling against my hair.

The cool night air hit my face as he carried me down the walkway. My head resting against his chest. The deep thud of his heart steadying me until my eyes were able to remain open.

"Koda?" My voice came out low and weak.

"Yeah, I got you. You passed out for a moment," he said, carefully sitting me in the passenger seat of his car. "Are you ok, Zaya?"

Before I could process what was happening, the front door swung open.

"Zaya?!?!" Jhovan's voice boomed through the front yard. He jogged down the steps, eyes darting from me to Koda. "Ayy man, who the fuck are you?"

Koda straightened, his jaw clenching and tight but he was calm. "Just someone who saw her struggling with luggage and bags. I was checking to see if she was ok. Then she collapsed on the grass. I was just trying to help." He said evenly.

"Help!?!?" Jhovan barked, his face twisting. "You've got your damn hands all over my wife!!"

"Then maybe you should've been the one catching her," Koda replied. His words hung heavy in the air.

I reached for the car door, voice shaking. "Jhovan, stop...please. I just got dizzy. This man didn't do anything wrong. He only tried to help me."

Jhovan puffed his chest out, eyes flicking from me back to Koda. "You need to come inside, Zaya."

"I'm not going anywhere with you," I whispered.

Koda moved closer, protective but controlled. "She needs air. Space. Let her breathe, man."

For a moment, no one moved. The streetlight flickered above us, and it gave me the feeling like things were about to go bad. In all the horror movies I'd watched, it always did.

Breaking the silence, Jhovan muttered, "Fuck it then. Stay out here and fall out again for all I care. I'm going back inside." He turned towards the house, slamming the door so hard it rattled the frame.

Koda exhaled slowly. "Seriously, Zaya. Are you ok?"

"I'm fine but I'll be even better when I get my kids."

"Ok, hop in. I'll take you." He offered.

"No, I think I need to drive my own car. How else would I get around if I don't?"

"I'll take my Harley, and you can drive the Chevelle or the Benz that's parked in my garage. You haven't seen that one. The point is, you will have something to drive. I normally wouldn't push the issue, but you passed out right in front of me. Most people don't pass out for no reason. Something serious may be going on."

"You're right. Something serious is going on. My life... my life is a fucking mess right now. I'm a bit overwhelmed but I really think I'm ok to drive."

"If you insist, I can't stop you, but I will trail behind you."

"Ok, that works and thank you again for being there. I told you my life was fuckery and you're getting a front row seat to it."

"It's not as bad as it could be, Zaya. Always remember that. Enough of the pep talk. Go ahead and get your behind in that SUV and let's go before he comes out that house again. I don't want to have to turn back into that man my father tried to tell you about."

I chuckled a little and headed to my SUV. Koda, picked the luggage and bags from the yard and loaded them into my trunk before running back to his car.

Tears blurred my eyes as I buckled myself in. I couldn't tell if it was fear, relief or both. I backed out the driveway and started up the road with Koda trailing behind me. As I pulled up to Jhovan's mama's house, I felt a hollow in my chest the moment I saw the porch light come on. My hands were trembling as I walked to the door.

"Mama Stone," I said. "Did Jhovan call you to let you know I was on the way?"

"He did but I'm trying to figure out what kind of shit y'all got going on over there?"

"Listen, I don't have time to discuss that right now. Maybe later but it's getting late and I have to situate my kids for school tomorrow. If you don't mind, I'd like to get them and leave."

She tilted her head, staring like I'd said something crazy. Just then, the kids came to the door with their backpacks, phones and Ipad in their hands.

"Oh, Hey Mama," Trinity said. "I thought we were staying with grandma for the night but I'm glad you came and got us."

"Hey Sugar, yall go ahead and get in the car and make

sure you put those seatbelts on. They filed into the back-seat, small bodies adjusting to the space like they belonged.

Mama Stone lingered on the porch. Phone already in her hand dialing numbers. "Umm, who's that in the car behind you?"

"Oh, his name is Koda. I had a little accident back at the house and he agreed to follow me here to make sure I was ok. Thank you for getting the babies for us. I will see you later." I turned and sauntered back to my SUV. When I looked back, I could see Mama Stone putting the phone to her ear before she closed the door.

Before I could put the car in reverse, my phone buzzed.

"Zaya, you need to stop this stupid shit you've got going on and bring your ass home. Where the fuck are you taking my children and why is that nigga still following you?" His voice low and fierce. The kind of voice that carried a promise of a storm. "I don't know who you think you're playing with but I'm serious. You better not hang up this phone...not at least until you get where you are going and you need to tell me where that is. I have a right to know where my children are," he growled.

"No, you have a right to know if they are safe or not and they are. Goodbye."

CHAPTER 14

Peace/No Peace

My stomach dropped, as I glanced in the rearview mirror at my children, blissfully unaware, laughing at something Thalia said. The tears were in full force by now, but I turned the volume up on the car stereo so they couldn't hear my sobs.

With Koda still behind me, I placed a call to him.

"I can't really talk, but I just need you on the phone with me. I need to calm down before my nose starts to bleed again. That would scare my babies and I'm not trying to do that. Koda, my nerves are so bad right now. I am literally shaking."

"I know they are, Zaya," he retorted. "You're going to be fine. I knew you wouldn't stay at my home with me, so while you were speaking to your husband's mother, I arranged a place for you and the kiddos. It's in my name...

this way he won't find you, and before you say anything, no, you can't pay me back and no, I didn't mind doing it. I will come and help you get the luggage from the car, make sure you and the kids are settled in, and I'll take off... if that's what you want.

I know you've got to have some long, hard conversations tonight, but first thing in the morning, you're calling your lawyer and advising her of what happened. A trespassing or restraining order needs to be next."

"Can I really get a restraining order against him? He didn't do anything to me physically?"

"Yeah, but he's threatened you on several occasions. That's enough. I know a few judges personally. I will make sure it gets pushed through. You've got this, ok. We've got this. I'm not letting you go through this alone."

I couldn't do anything but weep.

"Now Zaya, I'm about to pass you because you are driving slow as a turtle, and you don't know where you're going, so just follow me."

"Don't talk about my driving. I'm trying to be careful. I mean, I do have a state trooper behind me that's been known to give crying women tickets." I chuckled.

"Go ahead and make your jokes, but I've told you, girl, you've got to let that go. See you in a minute, sweetie."

Just like that, my frown disappeared, and I was now

full on cheesing. He zoomed in front of us, and we cruised down the highway and into town.

We arrived at a huge condominium, one I'd passed by a thousand times and never paid attention to. He parked, then ran to my side of the car.

"Hey Zaya, can I talk to you for a minute?"

"Mama, who's that man?" Jr. asked.

"Jr, this is Mama's friend. His name is Mr. Koda. Say hello to Mr. Koda, everyone."

"Hello, Mr. Koda," they all said in unison.

Giggling, he muttered, "Hello Zaya's babies. I'm just going to talk to your mom for just a few minutes. I'm a nice man, and I promise it won't take long."

I stepped out of the car and walked a few feet away from my SUV. My babies have been known to ear hustle, and they didn't need to hear any parts of our conversation.

"Why are we here, Koda?"

"This is one of my favorite resorts. Before I moved to Destin, this is where I always stayed. I loved it so much that I bought one, and whenever family comes to town, this is where they stay. I also rent it out as an Airbnb to keep some extra income flowing in. Anyhow, it's a three-bedroom and more than enough space for you and the kids. You can stay here as long as you want, and if I recall correctly, your job is right up the street."

"Koda, you didn't have to do all this. I work now, I

could have afforded a hotel room or something, or I could have just gone to my old house in Florala."

"Yeah, and you would have been miserable. You told me your mom offered you the house, and you declined because you didn't want to drive that far. Problem solved. Now, I told the kids it would only take a few minutes, and the few minutes are up. You are on the nineteenth floor. You have an oceanfront view. The condo is equipped with everything you need. Here," he handed me a post-it. "The codes to everything on the property are on that piece of paper, so don't lose it. Also, there are four wristbands to use any facility they offer," he handed me those as well. "Go on up and get settled. Would you like me to get a trolley for you?"

"That would be nice, Koda. Thank you so much." I smiled.

"Don't mention it."

As he walked to get a luggage cart, I went back to the SUV, grabbed the kids, and stood under the overhang. Koda returned with the trolley, and we all piled onto the elevator.

"Mama, are we going on vacation? A classmate of mine says her family stays in places like this when they go on vacation," Thalia questioned.

"Not exactly a vacation, baby, but more like a little getaway. Don't worry. It will be fun, ok? Plus, Mama has to have a talk with you all once we get settled. Not tonight though, maybe tomorrow. Once we get in this place, I want you all to get your clothes out for tomorrow, get your baths, and get straight to bed. Do you all understand?"

"Yes, but is daddy coming on our getaway too?"

"No, baby, and we will talk about that further but not tonight, ok?"

"Ok," they said.

The elevator door opened, and Koda stepped off first, leading the way. We arrived at unit 1907. Sleek black numbers glinted against a whitewashed door. He entered the code, pushed it open, and stepped aside so we could walk in first.

The second I crossed the threshold, the smell of the ocean hit me—not loud, but faint, as if someone had just closed the patio door.

My breath caught. The condo was stunning. It was bright, open, and superbly decorated. Wide glass doors stretched across the living room, revealing the ocean in all its glory. He walked over and opened the patio door. The sheer curtains swayed gently in the breeze, and the faint scent of salt and citrus drifted in from the balcony.

Whitewashed floors gleamed beneath my feet, and everything inside carried soft, coastal warmth. It featured beige, ivory and blue furniture, woven textures, and just enough color to feel alive. An ocean-blue sectional wrapped around a glass coffee table filled with seashells, and a large abstract painting of waves hung on the far wall. The kitchen flowed effortlessly into the space...all marble countertops, gold fixtures, and rattan barstools that looked too perfect to touch.

"Mama, look!" Trinity darted toward the balcony doors, pressing her tiny palms against the glass. "You can see the whole beach from here!"

I smiled, blinking back another wave of tears. "I see, baby. Don't go out on that balcony yet... let Mama catch her breath first."

Koda's voice came from behind me, low and easy. "The bedrooms are down that hallway. There are two on the left, master on the right. The main bathroom has a big soaking tub, and the kids' rooms already have fresh linens. I had a renter just leave last week, so the cleaners have already come through."

I turned to face him, my throat tightening. "You thought of everything, didn't you?"

He shrugged, offering that small, crooked smile that always seemed to calm me. "You've had enough chaos. You deserve a little peace."

For a moment, I didn't know what to say. The words tangled somewhere between gratitude and disbelief. "Koda... thank you. I mean it."

Trinity's little voice rang out from the hallway. "That's right. Thank you, Mr. Koda." We both cackled.

"I told you they be ear hustling," I laughed.

"Stop thanking me," he said softly, eyes warm. "Just breathe. Get the kids settled. Let the ocean do the rest."

"And you're welcome, Trinity," he said as he flashed her a warm smile.

I exhaled, deep and slow.

The kids ran down the hallway, their laughter echoing through the condo as I stepped toward the balcony, watching the waves crash against the shore. Behind me, I could hear Koda unloading luggage from the trolley, moving quietly, like he didn't want to disturb the moment.

"Don't look down too long. You may get dizzy again."

"It's so beautiful. I can't help it."

"My job is done here for the night. The rest is all yours. I want you to reach out if anything else happens. Remember, I'm only a phone call away."

"I would say thank you for everything, but you've already told me to stop, so I'll just say I appreciate you."

Nodding, he headed toward the door, and just like that, he was gone.

. . .

THE NEXT MORNING, I tried to do what I always did: breathe, get dressed, and pretend life wasn't falling apart. I took the kids to school, watched them run inside, and sat in the parking lot longer than I should have, staring at the steering wheel. My stomach felt like a fist. I was supposed to be fine. Koda said I would be fine.

By the time I reached my office, my hands were still trembling. I forced a smile at the receptionist, mumbled a good morning, and hurried to my workspace.

The studio smelled of eucalyptus and fresh paint, normally soothing, but not today. Sunlight streamed through the tall windows, bouncing off sample boards filled with soft coastal tones and minimalist furniture mock-ups. I was supposed to be finishing a layout for a client's beach cottage, but the letters on my computer screen swam in and out of focus.

I pressed a hand to my chest and whispered, Just work, Zaya. Just work.

I'd barely made it through one email before my phone lit up again... Jhovan.

I ignored it.

It rang again. And again.

The text messages came next.

> Jhovan: You think I'm stupid?

> Jhovan: Don't forget whose name is on everything.

Jhovan: You better answer me before I
pull up.

I froze. My head instantly began to throb.

"Zaya?" My assistant, Raina, peeked her head in. "You okay?"

I nodded quickly. "Yeah, just... just working through a design issue."

She hesitated before closing the door.

I picked up my phone and called Koda.

He answered on the first ring. "You made it to work?"

"Yes, I'm here." I sighed.

"Are you ok?"

"Yes, I'm fine. Just wanted to hear your voice."

There was silence on the other end, then his voice dropped an octave. "You don't sound fine."

"He's calling me nonstop. I blocked him, but he's using his work phone now. I'm fine, I promise. Just... I'm just a little shaken."

"Koda??"

"I'm coming up there."

Before I could protest, he hung up. I tried to focus again, but my nerves were shot. Ten minutes later, the sound of tires screeching outside made me jump. I peered out the window, and there he was.

Jhovan.

He slammed the car door and raced toward the entrance, phone in hand, jaw locked tight. My coworkers at the front desk looked up, startled, as he pushed through the door.

"Zaya!" His voice thundered through the office. "You think you can ignore me?"

Everyone turned. Conversations stopped.

I stood up quickly from my desk and walked toward the front of the building. My heart was pounding in my ears.

"Jhovan, stop! You cannot be here. This is my job... this is where I work. Please don't come here starting trouble."

"Don't tell me where the fuck I can or can't be," he snapped, closing the distance between us. "You disappear with my kids, got some stranger popping up and shit, and you think I wouldn't find out? You think I'm stupid, don't you? All you bitches in here think I'm stupid don't you?"

"Keep your voice down!" I hissed. "You're embarrassing yourself."

He laughed coldly. "Embarrassing myself? Oh, now I'm embarrassing myself? You're the one running around with another man behind my fucking back! Where did your whore ass take my kids last night? Where are you staying?"

Before I could reply, another voice cut through the chaos, firm and steady but calm.

"Step away from her."

His uniform was crisp... dark blue pressed pants, matching shirt with the silver badge glinting beneath the lights. The second he entered, the room went still. His presence demanded it.

"Sir," his voice was level but cold, "I'm going to need you to step back from her."

Jhovan turned, sneering. "Oh, it's you again. I knew I wasn't crazy. You must be the man she's fucking. So you a cop?"

Koda's jaw flexed. "State Trooper. And I don't think you want to test me right now."

"Man, you got no business here. This is between me and my wife, so you can get the fuck on."

"Correction," Koda said quietly, "this is between you and the law if you don't back up."

They locked eyes.

My coworkers started whispering. India was at the front, reaching for the office phone.

Jhovan took a step forward. "You think because you're in a uniform, I'm supposed to be scared? Man, fuck you. You can't protect her forever."

Koda's posture shifted slightly, still calm, but his voice hardened. "And that's just what I needed to hear. You threatened her in front of law enforcement. You aren't a smart one at all, are you?"

Jhovan and Koda stood chest to chest, tension thicker than a rope.

"Please," I yelled out, "stop! Jhovan, just leave!"

"Zaya, go back," Koda ordered, never removing his eyes from Jhovan's body.

"Oh, so you do what his weak ass tells you to do, but I don't get anything but backtalk. You know what... Fuck you, Zaya. Let's see how well you do with taking care of the kids by your damn self. Fuck you. You might as well get his ass to help you, cause I'm not doing shit else. You don't want to be with me no more... cool. Me and my bitches will live life to the fullest. I not looking back either."

The police arrived seconds later, moving toward Koda and Jhovan cautiously. They grabbed Jhovan's arm, steering him toward the exit.

Jhovan bucked free, scowling at me. "You're gonna regret this shit, Zaya. I promise you that. On everything I love... you're gonna regret it."

Koda's tone hardened, his voice cutting through the chaos. "That's enough. You're done here."

The police finally ushered him out, his threats fading down the hall. The moment the door closed behind them, the entire office seemed to deflate. The silence that followed was deafening, but the whole office was exhaling. From my peripheral, I could see Sylvia in the corner looking mortified with her mouth wide open.

Koda turned to me then, his expression softening. "You okay?"

I nodded weakly, tears threatening to flow. "I didn't think he'd actually show up here."

"I did," Koda murmured. "That's why I came. I've seen situations like this go sideways fast."

I pressed a hand to my mouth, trembling. "I can't live like this, Koda. My babies..."

"You need a domestic order specialist. I have one you can call." He reached into his shirt pocket and handed me a card. "They'll walk you through everything you need. But you should call your lawyer asap."

I nodded, already dialing her number.

"Altunia? It's me," I said when she answered, my voice cracked. "I need to file a restraining order. Today. I can't wait anymore. I have to protect myself and my kids."

As she began listing what to bring and where to go, I looked out the window, wondering what my days to come had in store.

CHAPTER 15

A Dream Is A Wish...

As I walked through the courthouse doors, a feeling of dread covered me. The smell of paper, coffee, and bad decisions permeated the air. Everything about it felt heavy. The sound of heels clicking, the quiet murmurs of people waiting to be called, and the long hallways that seemed to stretch on forever. I stood at the front counter, clutching a clipboard full of forms my lawyer had emailed me to fill out before I arrived.

Koda was beside me, silent, a firm presence that somehow made the noise fade. His uniform drew attention. Heads turned when he walked through, but he didn't seem to notice. He'd told me he'd accompany me "just to make sure it all went smoothly," but I knew better. He was making sure I didn't have to face this alone, and I was grateful.

The clerk slid the paperwork across the counter.

"Mrs. Stone, once you finish this section, take it to courtroom three on the second floor. The judge is hearing protective order requests today. You'll be called when it's your turn."

"Thank you," I whispered.

I took a seat on a wooden bench, the pen trembling in my fingers as I filled in the last blanks. Threats, Harassment, Intimidation, Jhovan's name, address, and any incidents I could recall. The words blurred a few times from tears I couldn't wipe away fast enough. Each line hurt to write, but I did it anyway. Because I had to.

When I was done, I looked up at Koda. "It feels like I'm turning my whole life into evidence."

He met my gaze, steady and sure. "You're not turning your life into evidence, Zaya. You're taking control of it."

I swallowed hard and nodded.

The waiting felt endless. When my name was finally called, my legs had gone stale, like they weren't mine anymore.

The courtroom was smaller than I expected, with just a few rows of benches, a judge's bench elevated slightly, and a court clerk typing quietly beside him. My lawyer, Altunia, met me at the front, her voice low and reassuring.

"You're doing great," she murmured. "Just answer honestly. The judge is fair."

I nodded, glancing back at Koda. He stood near the back wall, hands folded neatly in front of him, watching me like he could will me strength from across the room.

The judge looked over his glasses as I approached. "Mrs. Stone, I've reviewed your petition. It states that you've received multiple threats from your husband, including in-person confrontations and excessive calls and messages. Is that correct?"

"Yes, sir," I said softly.

He motioned for me to continue. "Tell me, in your own words, what's been happening."

I took a deep breath. "It started small...arguments that got louder, messages that turned into threats. He turned especially angry when he found out I knew he was cheating and didn't confront him about it. I guess he wanted me to be upset, but I wasn't. I was relieved because I wanted out. I told him last night that I was leaving him, and that's when he threatened me inside my own home. He'd been acting a little crazy. I didn't want me or my kids to have to deal with that, so I left. This morning, he came to my job and acted a fool. Everyone in my office is now terrified and so am I. He's become unpredictable, and I'm scared he's going to do something to me that I can't come back from."

The judge's gaze softened, but his tone stayed firm. "Do you believe you and your children are in danger?"

My voice cracked. "From his actions last night and this morning, yes. I do."

He nodded once, then turned to the clerk. "Temporary restraining order granted. Effective immediately. Respondent is prohibited from contacting the petitioner or her minor children in any way, directly or indirectly. Sheriff's department will serve notice today."

I let out a breath I hadn't realized I was holding.

"Thank you," I whispered, clutching the edge of the table.

When it was over, I stepped into the hallway and fell into Koda's arms, covering my face with my hands as the tears fell. I wasn't crying because I was sad, not even because I was scared, but from exhaustion, relief, and the crushing reality that this was really happening.

Koda whispered gently in my ear, "You did it."

I laughed through the tears, shaking my head. "I can't believe it. It doesn't feel real."

"It will," he said softly. "It'll start to feel lighter, one day at a time."

I looked up at him and saw not just the man who was constantly coming to my rescue, but the man behind the badge. The one who'd seen too many bad endings and was determined to make sure mine didn't end that way.

He tilted his head. "You ready to go?"

I nodded. "Been ready."

We walked out together, the courthouse doors opening to bright sunlight. The world looked the same, but my spirit felt a bit lighter. Cars were passing by, people were laughing, and in the breeze, I could smell salt in the air. Things were shifting, and I was standing my ground.

It was still early when court let out. I placed a call to my mother to give her an update on her son-in-law before heading back to the condo.

"Hey, Mama."

Her voice came through soft but urgent. "Baby, I've been waiting on your call. You alright?"

My voice trembled. "I'm okay. It's been a long twenty-four hours."

She sighed, the sound full of knowing. "So, tell me what's going on."

"I just left the courthouse. I had to file a restraining order on Jhovan. He started acting crazy when the kids and I returned from your house, and he...he just wouldn't stop. He started threatening me, but he really crossed the line when he came up to my job acting a fool." I rubbed at my temple. "I just... I can't believe it's come to this."

"Well, believe it, Zaya. You did what you had to do."

There was a pause...the kind that comes when you have something to say but don't quite know how to navigate it.

"I'll go get the kids today. You need time to reflect,

baby," Mama finally said. "Don't you worry about them. I'll pack some things, pick them up from school, and take them down to the house in Florala. They can stay there a few days until you get your mind settled."

I sat up straighter. "Mama, are you sure? They've got school --"

She cut me off gently. "It won't hurt for them to miss a few days. I'll stop by the school, talk to their teachers, and get their homework. I'll make sure they don't fall behind."

The relief hit me so hard my eyes stung. "Thank you, Mama."

"Don't thank me, baby. Thank God." Her voice softened, the way it always did when she was about to say something deeper. "I had a dream about all this, you know."

I blinked. "A dream?"

"Mmm-hmm," she responded.

Here it comes. Mama never missed, so I listened closely.

"I saw you standing in the middle of the road," she said slowly. "It was stormin' so bad I could barely see you, and there were cars passing by you on each side. You didn't move; you just stood there. I was on the porch screaming, telling you to get out the road before you got hit by a car, but you didn't budge. I ran, trying to get to you, but when I looked up again...there was a man...tall, dark, standing beside you, holding an umbrella over your head. The rain wasn't touching you, Zaya, and neither did those cars. Not a single drop. I knew then that God had sent somebody to cover you."

I swallowed hard. "You're talking about Koda?"

"That's exactly who I'm talking about," she said firmly. "That man is your angel on earth. Don't push him away trying to prove you can handle everything alone."

"I don't, Mama. He won't let me. He's always there when I need him, and even when I think I don't."

"Good, cause sometimes, strength looks like letting somebody help you stand."

As I pulled into the condo parking lot, tears slid down my cheeks before I could stop them. Still on the phone with Mama, Koda and I trekked to the elevator and to the door. I entered, kicked off my shoes, and headed toward the balcony. I stared out at the ocean that seemed endless.

"I don't even know how to tell the kids they can't see their father," I whispered.

"I know, baby. But you'll find the words when it's time. Right now, just rest. Let me handle everything else."

Her tone was final, loving, unshakeable...like it always was when she took over.

"Okay," I murmured. "Call me when you get to Florala?"

"I will. And Zaya?"

"Yes, Mama?"

"Don't let that fear back in your life. You're leaving it behind for a reason."

I hung up and sat there for a long time, staring at the waves until the blur of sunlight and tears melted together.

Behind me, I heard Koda's voice from the kitchen. "Coffee's ready, if you're up for it."

I turned, wiped my face, and managed a small smile. "Yeah," I said softly. "I think I am."

"So, how are you and the kids liking the place so far? Is it up to par? I know it's not like the mini mansion you live in, but it's nice, yeah?"

"It's more than nice, Koda. I love it, and the kids love it, but you know I don't plan on staying here long. I need to get my own place. My plan was to have enough to move out before I filed papers, but his actions sped that process up real quick. I don't think I could have gone another day in that house without killing someone."

"Well, you know what they say. God laughs when we make plans."

"Yes, he does, Koda. I needed this, all of this. The silence, the peace, and the freedom. It's weird," I said softly. "I thought I'd feel... triumphant, or relieved. But I just feel... empty. Like I've been cheating myself out of the life I've wanted for years. Now, I have a chance at it, and I feel like I can't breathe."

Koda leaned against the counter across from me, still in uniform. "That's normal," he said simply. "You're going through a lot right now. Shit, if you ask me...divorcing someone you once loved is traumatizing. It's like a death, and for some people, it breaks them. You aren't letting it break you, and I'm proud of you for that. It's ok to be upset and confused. You are allowed to feel what you feel. Just know the relief comes later. After your central nervous system realizes it's safe. That takes time."

Safe.

That word hit something deep in me.

I looked at him. "You make it sound so simple," I said with a tired smile.

He shrugged slightly. "Yeah, but simple doesn't mean easy."

I stood to return back into the condo, and the weight of the day came crashing down. "I think I'm gonna lie down for a bit," I murmured.

He nodded toward the bedroom. "Go ahead. You know where it is."

But when I started walking that way, I paused. "Will you--" I hesitated, feeling ridiculous. "Will you just... stay close? I don't know why, but the quiet feels too loud right now."

"Sure. I'll be right here."

I went into the bedroom, peeled off my blazer, and sat

on the edge of the bed. Through the cracked door, I could see Koda moving through the condo, methodical and calm. Taking off his duty belt, placing his hat on the hook by the door, checking the locks once, twice.

When I finally laid down, exhaustion pulled me under fast. The sound of the ocean outside the window was the last thing I heard... that, and the quiet creak of a chair as Koda settled in the living room to keep watch.

As I got comfortable and began to snooze, my phone rang. Pamela's face flashed across the screen.

I answered, and she started in with, "Bitch, what the fuck is going on with your husband? Is he on some kind of meds or something? Because if not, he needs to be."

"What are you talking about, Pamela?" I asked, still half asleep.

"Wake the fuck up, Zaya. Jhovan was just brought in for processing, and he is acting a damn fool. What happened?"

"He's in there, so I'm sure you can figure it out?"

"Bitch, don't get smart with me again. I don't have time to read no damn paperwork. Tell me what he did."

"Girl, so much has happened in these few days, and to make a long story short... He threatened me in front of everyone at my job, including Officer Williams, and the police took his ass to jail. I just left the courthouse getting that restraining order you recommended. He's mad because he can't get to me. Girl, that man had gone crazy. Please keep his ass in there as long as you can."

"Zaya, I'm not a judge, lawyer, or even a correctional officer. I have no control over that."

"Can't you pad his file or something?" I chuckled.

"Girl, if I didn't think my ass would get caught...I would. Hell, I wouldn't have known he was in here if he wasn't showing his entire ass. He saw me and really turned up. He mentioned something about me hooking you up with one of my partners. Then he called me a skeezer and a trout mouth ass bitch," she chuckled. "I started to taze his big ass."

"I'm so sorry bestie, but that is what he does these days. Go clean off and doesn't stop. Anyway, friend, my children and I are good, but I'm tired as hell. My mental is so drained from all this shit. I'll be glad when it's all over. Oh, and I filed my divorce. Before you say anything, I told you a lot has happened in these few days."

"I know you are doing what you have to do. I know you're tired so I'll let you go. I was just calling to check on you to make sure you were ok. I love you, friend, and please keep me posted."

"Love you too and will do."

I hung up, thinking about my mother's dream, then I slipped into my own. Finally, I slept without fear.

CHAPTER 16

Be Still My Heart

The gravel crunched under my tires as I turned into the long, winding driveway that led to Mama's house. It sat on a quiet stretch of land just outside Florala. The air felt different here. It was slower, lighter, cleaner somehow.

As soon as I parked, I spotted my babies in the yard. Thalia was chasing Jr. around the oak tree while little Trinity sat in the grass with a crown of wildflowers on her head. They looked so carefree, like nothing in the world could touch them.

Mama came out onto the porch, drying her hands on a dish towel. "Told you they'd be fine," she said with a smile.

I got out of the car and met her halfway, wrapping my arms around her before I even spoke. "I didn't realize how much I missed this place," I whispered in her ear.

She kissed my cheek. "Home has a way of reminding you who you are."

Inside, the house smelled like cornbread and potpourri, her two favorite things. Old gospel records played in the background, and sunlight peeked through lace curtains.

"Sit," she said, motioning to the table. "I made you some tea. Chamomile with honey... you look like you need it."

I sat, my shoulders finally sinking. "How have they been?"

"Girl, you act like you haven't seen them in weeks. It's only been three days," she said, pulling out a chair across from me. "They are good, baby. Quiet. They've asked a few questions, but I told them Mama needed a little time to rest her mind."

I sighed. "They deserve better than all this."

Mama reached across the table and placed her hand over mine. "Zaya, you did what you had to do to keep them safe. Don't you start doubting that now."

The screen door creaked open and Thalia peeked in. "Mama, can we stay another night? Nana said we could go to the lake tomorrow."

"Of course, baby," I said with a small smile. "Go play."

Once the door shut again, Mama gave me that look. The look that saw straight through me.

"You're still thinking about him," she said quietly.

I didn't bother denying it. "He's out of jail already. I blocked him, but he keeps calling from blocked numbers. Leaving messages I don't even play anymore. Mama, I don't know who he is anymore. He's definitely not the man I married."

She sat back, eyes soft but steady. "You know exactly who he is. You just stopped pretending not to see it."

My throat tightened because she was right... as always.

Mama got up and went to the counter, stirring her tea slowly. "The storm's not over yet, Zaya, but you're standing in a different place now. You've got peace covering you and God walking beside you. You'll be just fine."

I turned toward the window, watching the kids chase butterflies as dusk settled over the yard. Their laughter floated through the air, soft and pure. I wasn't doing this just for me, but for them as well. They deserve so much better than what he'd given them.

The evening breeze rolled in, carrying the scent of country pine and fresh-cut grass as headlights rolled down the long driveway. I looked up from the porch swing just as Koda's cruiser came into view, dust trailing behind it. My heart did that little thing again.

Mama followed my gaze, setting her glass of freshly

made sweet tea on the table. "That your state trooper?" she asked, her tone half-curious, half-knowing.

I laughed softly. "He's not my state trooper, Mama. He's the state of Florida's State Trooper"

"Mmhmm," she hummed, clearly unconvinced.

The car door opened and Koda stepped out, tall and composed, his uniform catching the last light of day. He tipped his hat as he approached the porch. "Evening, Ms. Harper. I'm Koda Williams. I just wanted to check in on Zaya and the kids, make sure everyone's settling in all right."

Mama eyed him up and down. Not in a rude way... just reading him like only mothers can. "So, you're the one that's been looking out for my daughter."

"Yes, ma'am," he said simply. "Just doing what anyone would."

She chuckled, folding her arms. "Don't give me that. Most folks turn their head when they see a woman falling apart. You didn't."

Koda's jaw tensed a little. "I've seen too many women not make it out. I couldn't stand by and watch it happen again."

That answer softened something in her. She motioned toward the porch. "Well, come on up, son. No sense in standing out there like you're still on duty."

He climbed the steps, his boots creaking against the

wood. I could tell he was a little nervous, which made me smile.

Mama poured him a glass of tea and slid it over. "You got good eyes, officer," she said after a long pause. "You see things before they happen, don't you?"

Koda nodded slowly. "I try to."

She smiled faintly. "Good. 'Cause I had a dream and in it, I saw my daughter crying, then resting, then finally laughing again. But she wasn't alone. There was a man beside her, and peace was all around them. When I woke up, I told myself: that man must be her angel on earth."

Koda blinked fast, caught off guard. "Ma'am, I don't know about all that."

"Oh, you don't have to know," Mama said with a grin. "Just keep showing up."

I looked between them, warmth radiating in my chest. I was finally starting to feel like everything was exactly where it needed to be.

5 Months Later

Spring rolled into summer, and the world began to bloom again. So did I.

The kids had fallen into a new rhythm between school, therapy, and weekends at the beach. I'd taken on more design clients, pouring my heart into projects that reflected peace and color...the things I'd once forgotten I loved. I also found myself and the kids a nice three-bedroom house minutes away from their school and my job. Things were going well, and through it all, Koda was there.

Sometimes he'd stop by my office with lunch, still in uniform, that soft smile lighting up the room. Other times, he'd come over to my house to hang out with me and the kids. He loved to grill burgers on the patio and help Jr. fix his toy trucks. He'd even brought his father up a time or two.

It wasn't rushed or forced. Just... natural. Easy.

A quiet understanding built between us, one that didn't need labels.

One warm Friday morning, I stood in my office, flipping through fabric samples, when my phone buzzed with an email from my lawyer.

Subject: Final Decree of Divorce – Signed and Filed.

For a moment, I couldn't move. My hands shook, my eyes filling with tears that burned but didn't hurt. I screamed, "It's over."

Sylvia bolted into my office. "What's going on in here? Are you ok?" she asked.

"Yes. I'm better than ok. I'm finally divorced. I am fucking free. I'm free," I yelled.

Sylvia stood in the door smiling, shaking her head.

"Listen, I know you hate my guts and all, but I want

you to know I'm really happy for you, girl. I truly am. I remember feeling the exact same way when my divorce was final. Shit, you should have a party or something. Getting away from him needs to be celebrated. Especially if it could compare to his actions in the office that day. I didn't know whether to hide for cover or take off running."

I laughed. "Yeah, he was really on some other shit that day but it's over now. And Sylvia, I forgive you for hooking me up with him," I winked and we cracked up laughing.

She whispered, "You think you can forgive me for that other thing too?"

I pondered her question for a few seconds before muttering, "Yes, that thing too. I was just so hurt. You were one of my only friends here, Sylvia, and for you to betray me like that really broke me."

"I'm sorry, Zaya. I run my mouth too much, especially when I'm drinking. I should have never told Kevin about the abortion, but I had no idea he would go back and tell Jhovan," she admitted.

"Sylvia, if you saw how he reacted when he found out, you would understand why I was so pissed. He cried and cried for days. Then went quiet on me. It was weeks before he spoke to me again. He heard abortion and lost his mind. I did my best to explain that it wasn't an elected abortion but an emergency. The baby was in my tubes and could have killed me. He didn't want to hear that shit. All he kept saying was, 'You killed my seed'." It was terrible. Anyhow, that's all old news and it's fine...well, now it is. Life is too short to hold on to grudges, so yes, I forgive you."

She ran in for a hug, and I gave her the stiff arm.

"Hold on now. That's too soon, too fast. You've got to give me some time. You've got too much dip on your chip, Sylvia." She backed away and laughed as she left my office.

I finished up for the day and headed out the door. Grabbing my purse, I drove to the beach and stood barefoot in the sand, letting the waves wash over my toes and talking to God. Every ounce of me felt lighter... unshackled.

I called everyone with ears to tell them I was free, but the first person was my mother.

"Mama, guess what?"

"What, child? I don't have time to be guessing. My stories are on," she muttered.

"My divorce is final. The papers came back a couple of hours ago. Mama, I did it."

"Yes, baby, you did." I could feel her smile through the phone. "This is your new beginning. No looking back, only forward. Now, you can finally lay into that fine ass 'friend' of yours. That man is fine, fine. I know you've been waiting to get it on, and I don't blame you. Y'all need to go out somewhere and celebrate. I tell you what, Zaya. Why don't you head down to his place, and I'll get the kids from school. They can spend the weekend with me."

"You don't have to do that, Mama. It's not necessary."

"I know what I don't have to do, but I want to do this. I want you to process what you've been through, what's in store, then celebrate. I see nothing but good times ahead for you and Koda," her voice low but serious.

"I love you, Mama, and thank you."

"Thank me by enjoying your weekend. Come pick them up Sunday after church. Now, bye."

I sat around for the rest of the day, basking in the glow of being a single woman. I wanted to celebrate in more ways than one, so I placed a call to Pamela to see what she was up to.

She answered on the first ring.

"Where are you, hooker?"

"At home, about to watch a new show I found on the ID network. Why... what's up?"

"My papers came in today. I am officially a divorced woman. I wanted to go by the liquor store and get a bottle of D'usse. I feel like taking a few shots to the head. Do you feel like celebrating with me?"

"Hell yeah, get that bottle and I'll bring mine over. Give me thirty minutes and I'll be there because if anyone needs to celebrate their divorce...it's your ass."

Within twenty minutes, Pamela arrived at my door, and she was ready to drink. My good sis must have had a long week as well. We danced, laughed, and partied like there was no tomorrow. We made it an early night. Pamela was back on morning shift and had to report to work at 6:00 A.M. She needed to get back home early enough to sleep it off.

After she left, I took a ride to Koda's house. He greeted me at the door with champagne and that crooked grin I adored. "To new beginnings," he said, clinking his glass against mine.

"To peace," I replied.

"Now that this whole thing with your ex-husband is over, I would love nothing more than to handcuff you to my bed and fuck you until you pass out."

I clutched my invisible pearls. "Well damn, Officer Williams...where did that come from? This is my type of carrying on," I moved in closer and licked him across the lips.

"Zaya, you have no idea of the amount of restraint I use when I'm near you. I've kept it respectful because you were a married woman, but you aren't anyone's wife now. You are no longer his. You're mine and I'm going to make love to you like we've shared the last ten lifetimes together. The shit I'm going to do to you could have me arrested in at least thirty states."

One look in his eyes and I could tell he wasn't playing around. He took my champagne glass from my hand, set it on the coffee table and led me to the bedroom. The second we entered, I unbuckled his belt and dropped to my knees. Taking him into my mouth, he bucked and shuddered like my mouth was made of fire. I circled his dick with my tongue, licking from the shaft to the tip. I cuffed and licked his balls too. Being sure to give them their own attention.

"Look at me," I said as I slowly made his dick disappear. As I came up for air, I whispered, "Don't take your eyes off me." Grabbing his swollen member, I took it into my mouth again. This time, I played the trumpet with his dick. Milking while I spit and slurped. His knees buckled.

He looked down at me with the most beautiful grimace I'd ever seen. Pleasure etched across his face.

"Fuuuuuuck, Zaya. You got to slow down baby. I haven't had none in close to a year. You gone fuck around and make me cum too fast." He groaned.

"It's ok if you do, baby. The kids are gone for the whole weekend. We've got time," I said as I kissed the head gently before I continued licking, sucking and slurping.

Grabbing the back of my head, he guided my mouth up and down on his shaft.

"Get your hands off me, I'm running this show. This is my dick...let me handle it the way I see fit." I ordered.

"Gyaaaat Damn, Zaya. Shit girl..you sucking the shit out that muthafucka. I can't...."

"You can't what, Koda. Say it," I quipped.

"I...I can't hold it. I'm about to cum.." he grunted.

"No, you're not. You aren't about to cum are you?" I asked as I continued stretching my jaws to accommodate his width. He was huge and his shit was throbbing with each heartbeat.

"Yes, Zaya...Yes...I'm a.....bout....to...cummmm." He said as he pulled his dick from my mouth just as it started to erupt like a volcano. I swatted his hand away. Taking it back into my mouth and deep throating him until every drop slid down my throat. Gagging, I let it flop out, sliding it one last time across my lips. Koda stood there in awe, face balled up like he was in pain.

"Babe, are you ok?" I asked.

"I'm better than ok. Shiddd...your mouth should be illegal. What in the hell have I gotten myself into? Zaya, I'm going to be honest with you. No one has ever devoured my dick like that. Just in case you were wondering, yes, I love you. We can go get married tomorrow if you want," he chuckled.

"Damn girl...You didn't even let us get all the way out our clothes. I thought I was the one that's in control."

"I guess we see who's really running shit around here.

Just so you know, I'm a bit dominant in the bedroom but I don't mind taking an order or two."

"I see now, I'm really gonna need my cuffs. It's just my luck because here they are right here," he says as he raised them above his head.

"I don't know how I feel about those cuffs, Koda." I expressed.

"Do you not trust me? You should know by now, I would never do anything to hurt you. If I'm doing something that makes you uncomfortable, all you have to do is give me a safe word and I'll stop immediately."

"Damn, we about to get it in like that. Am I really going to need a safe word?"

"You may...too much pleasure can be painful sometimes." He said with that crooked smile.

"Ok. How about...Bubblegum."

"Bubblegum it is," he concurred. Now bring your ass over here," he said as he grabbed me by the waist and pulled me close to him.

The way he looked at me made it hard to breathe. It was like he saw every broken piece I'd tried to hide. He kissed me deeply. Tasting every ounce of me and I relished in it. I hadn't made love in what felt like ages, and I wanted nothing more than to make up for lost time.

"Still holding me by the waist, he gently stripped me piece by piece. I stood there naked before him...tiger stripes, cesarean scars all on display. He kneeled down before me and kissed each and every one.

Once insecure about my war wounds, none of that mattered in that moment. I'd never felt more beautiful. He raised my arms above my head then slapped the handcuffs on with one hand.

"I've dreamed about this moment for so long. Your body is even more beautiful than I'd imagined."

The damn broke in my yoni once again and from the first lick to my pussy. I knew the floodgates were about to open. His licks started soft, yet firm and within minutes, he was going full throttled. He pushed me back on the bed then planted his tongue between my slick folds again.

"Yes, Koda. Taste me." I moaned. "That feels so fucking good."

My moans fueled his intensity. He sucked my pussy so good, I found it difficult to keep my composure. So difficult that I forgot my safe word. I tried to back away but he grabbed me under my thighs and slid me to the edge of the bed. Not once coming up for air.

"Koda, please." I begged.

"Koda, please what. I'm not letting you go until my job is done. If you can talk, it's not done. I don't wanna hear shit but your moans."

He kept lapping at my pussy, then trickled down to my asshole. He licked and sucked my yoni like it was the sweetest nectar he'd tasted. He slid in a finger and continued flicking my clit. He had a serious tongue game, but I couldn't wait to experience that log in his pants. We'd kissed, groped and even fondle each other but this was our first time taking it there.

Finally, he came up for air. With his tongue, he explored every inch of my body. He kissed my neck ever so softly as he rubbed his fingers across my lips. My tongue found his mouth, and we kissed deep enough for our taste buds to become one. He smelled so good, spice mixed with a whole lotta man. Spreading my legs apart, he slid so deep into my center, my toes curled. Slowly, he stroked my pussy like he was savoring it. His grip was firm beneath my ass and the look on his face reflected what we both were feeling. Ecstasy.

"Ooh, Zaya. Baby, you're so tight." He moaned.

Using my muscles, I squeezed his dick with every stroke. "Yes, Koda....oooh baby. You're hitting my spot."

And he was.

It didn't take long before that tingle crawled up my spine. I knew it wouldn't be long before my release. I wanted to warn him about my squirting but figured it would be a welcome surprised. When the first wave of pleasure hit, my orgasm was so powerful that my muscles pushed him out then came the geyser.

He stared and me, then at my pussy, watching it

convulse as I pumped ounce after ounce from my center. He was amazed and looked at me with so much adoration. He couldn't wait to get back in. He slid back into my center, fueled from what he'd just seen and fucked me even harder. As he stroked me into an oblivion, the second wave came...this time, I pulled him in by the waist and let my love drip all over him. He didn't miss a beat, he continued stroking through the chaos and when he released, I felt the pressure hit my walls. What we shared was powerful, sensual and everything I'd imagined. He was well worth the wait.

He moaned, "I love you, Zaya," as he collapsed on top of me.

"I love you too, Koda," escaped from my mouth without a second thought.

CHAPTER 17

Aht Aht

3 WEEKS POST DIVORCE

I'd just come home from dropping the kids off at school, humming softly as I unlocked the door. The morning sun spilled across my living room as I put the tea kettle on the burner. Everything felt ordinary and peaceful... until it wasn't.

That chill hit first...a strange, heavy stillness that didn't belong.

I turned and froze.

Jhovan was standing in the corner of my living room, leaned against the wall like he'd been waiting. Arms folded, sunglasses hiding his eyes... but not that smirk.

A lump formed in my throat. He looked different. Thinner. Weaker. Like the months apart had carved the softness right out of him.

"Jhovan." My voice came out strained. I fumbled for my purse, heart pounding.

He pushed off the wall, slow and deliberate. Each step closed the space between us faster than I expected. I kept thinking... if only I could just get to my gun, I'd blow this bastard's head clean off his shoulders.

He interrupted my thoughts with a low, casual drawl:

"Been a long time, Zaya. This is a cute lil place you've got here. You think you can just erase me? File papers and pretend I never existed?"

"Jhovan, that's what you said you wanted. You said you would never look back, so why are you here? You need to get the fuck away from me." My throat was tight. "There's a restraining order—"

He laughed, a dark, broken sound that made my stomach twist.

"A piece of paper don't change what's real. You'll never not be mine."

I stepped back, pulse racing.

"If you don't leave, I'm calling—"

"Call him," he snapped, cutting me off mid-sentence.

"Call your trooper boyfriend. See if he can save you every time."

He moved closer. I could feel the heat from his body, smell the faint trace of cologne I used to love. His words were slow, almost delicate... yet his eyes were dark, shifty.

"You think you're free, Zaya. But you don't even know what I'm capable of. Oh, and tell my babies I'll see them later. We are going to go for a ride. If you're a good girl, I might let you tag along."

Then, just as suddenly, he turned and walked out. The sound of his tires echoed in my ears long after he was gone.

I stood frozen, heart pounding. My peace... shattered in seconds.

The tea kettle screamed behind me, mocking the normalcy that had existed just minutes before. That sound finally snapped me out of it. My first thought was to call Koda, but I didn't want or need him to come to my rescue this time. I was a bad bitch before either man—Jhovan or Koda—entered my life, and I sure as hell could be that again. Especially with my sanity and children at stake.

I trekked to the kitchen and poured tea because my hands needed something to do. The peppermint was almost scorching when I brought the cup to my lips. I sat down on the couch and replayed the discovery in a loop—the messages I shouldn't have seen, the panties, the smell of someone else on his shirts, the slippery excuses that had become his second skin.

Back then, I'd wanted revenge the way a fat kid wanted cake, but I'd talked myself out of it. I told myself I wanted out, not war. I wanted my life back, not a headline.

Now... the part of me that had been quiet for so long

unraveled like a black flag. It wasn't the same anger; it was focused... fiercer.

I set the cup down and let my fingers linger on the rim. I pictured him again, that cocky tilt of his head, the way he thought he could own me because he'd owned pieces of my life. I didn't close my eyes when the images came, and I didn't have to be asleep to see it. The vision was clear as day, just like that nagging that told me he was cheating.

I watched him choke on his own blood inconsolably. Bringing my tea cup to my lips, the almost scorching peppermint tea burned going down with a bittersweet taste—similar to watching him take his last breath. This vision made my jaw tighten with a cold kind of joy.

I shook off my thoughts and sent a quick text to Koda.

> Me: Can't wait to taste those soft, juicy lips on your face.

> Koda: And I can't wait to taste those lips below your waist.

I stared at the phone, smiling ear to ear despite what I'd just experienced. Although I knew I'd have to deal with it sooner than later, I didn't want to ruin the mood with talks of Jhovan. I'd eventually get around to it.

Koda was off today and was due to head over around 9-ish for a rump session. Since my divorce, we'd been fucking like rabbits, and I wasn't going to let my ex-husband ruin the momentum I had with my man.

While I waited, I called the non-emergency police number to report that he'd violated his restraining order. Since I was due at work in an hour or so, I told them I would come in shortly to file the report. I wanted it documented just in case I had to peel his shit back. I needed them to know I was doing my part by staying away from him. He wasn't doing the same.

I called a security company and made an appointment to have cameras installed throughout the entire house, including hidden ones. I checked my gun in my purse to make sure it was fully loaded. I also retrieved my other three from their safe, loaded them, and placed them in different areas of the home.

The look in Jhovan's eyes told me all I needed to know. Him mentioning our babies really didn't sit well with me. I called the school to advise once again that their father was no longer on the emergency or pick-up list, and that if he came for any reason, the school needed to call the police immediately. I wasn't taking any chances with this damn sicko. He'd lost more than his family, but apparently, his marbles too. The more I thought about it, the more anger coursed through my veins.

Without another thought, I called his mother.

She answered on the first ring.

"Zaya, well what do I owe the pleasure?" she said, slick as ever.

"Mother Stone, your son just left my house. He threatened me again. I'm giving you a courtesy call because if he comes near my house again...I'm going to blow his muthafuckin head off. This is his and yours first and last warning," I hissed.

"What did you say, little girl?" she gritted.

"I didn't stutter. You know I have a restraining order against him. He's not supposed to be within 500 feet of me or my children. He was standing in my fuckin living room when I got home this morning!!" I yelled.

"He threatened me yet again, then walked out like he was scaring somebody. I'm not scared of him. That's something he needs to know. He also needs to know I will do whatever I can to keep breathing. He's stated multiple times I'd regret leaving him and he would make me pay. I'm not trying to prove him right, so just know. I'm gunning for his head."

"Listen here, you bougie ass bitch. You haven't let my son see his kids in months. You filed a divorce out of nowhere and moved on before the ink was dry on the paper. I told his ass years ago he should have never married you. You were the worst thing to ever happen to him. My boy ain't been right since you came into his life. You've practically ruined his—"

I cut her off mid-sentence.

"There you go again, putting the blame on everyone but him. Jhovan is the reason why Jhovan is divorced. Jhovan is the reason why he can't see his kids. People like you are exactly what's wrong with him. Nobody holds his feet to the fire. Nobody tells him when he's wrong and makes him take accountability. I'm not about to go back and forth with you. Like I said, this was a courtesy call to tell you to get your black dress ready. Bye."

I was hanging up the phone just as Koda knocked on the door.

"Who were you fussing at, babe? I could hear you as I walked to the door."

"Koda, we don't have to talk about that," I said, kissing him on the neck and pulling him to the couch.

He pulled away.

"No, seriously, babe. Who was that on the phone? I've never heard you raise your voice without a reason. Not even when the kids are being mischievous. Tell me what's going on."

"Dang, ok then. Sit down." I huffed.

He did.

"Jhovan was here when I got back home this morning." I held my breath while he processed what I'd just said.

"Here, as in the driveway?" His brows furrowed but his voice was low and steady.

"No, babe. Here, as in standing in the corner right there," I pointed.

"Why aren't the police here taking your statement?" he questioned.

"Before you get all rowdy, I've taken care of it all. I called them to let them know already. I'm going in to give my statement before I head into the office. I also called the security company to have cameras installed. My guns are in place, and I'm good. Now, can we fuck, please?"

"Zaya, are you serious right now? You do not get to breeze past this. Tell me what he said."

I could see from the look in his eyes I wasn't getting any dick this morning, so I gave up.

"Koda, he said that I had a cute lil place and that the divorce didn't mean shit. He also told me to tell the kids he said hi and that he was going to take them on a ride or something like that. I can't remember exactly."

Koda's eyes got big as saucers.

"So wait, not only did he threaten you but the kids too? This muthafucka has seriously lost his shit. What was he driving, Zaya?"

"It was a car I'd never seen before. I noticed it parked across the street when I came home but didn't think anything about it. People are always parking over here. The beach is right up the street. Ummm, let me think. It was a slate grey Dodge. Not sure which model because I wasn't paying attention."

"You need to call the sch—," he muttered.

"Baby, I've done all that. I promise you, I've thought of it all. I'm okay. My kids are going to be okay. I'm sure of it. I'm taking every precaution I can to make sure nothing else happens. He caught me slipping this time, but I promise you, that won't happen again. Next time, and there will be a next time...I'll be ready."

Koda looked at me for a while before speaking.

"You know, if I didn't know any better, I'd think you were a crazy woman. Here you are, chilling all laid back on the couch like you don't have a care in the world. Like there isn't a damn madman on the loose."

"Koda, I can't control him. I can only control how I respond to him. I'm no longer going to ruin my own peace worried about Jhovan's ass, and if it means anything to you...I'd like to put this conversation to rest. Especially since you won't give me any of that good stuff."

"Maybe later, sweetheart, but my mind is elsewhere right now. It's where I thought yours would be after telling me what you told me. I think my calm may have rubbed off on you a little too much." He chuckled lightly as he stood up and headed to the door.

"Wait, we've still got a few minutes, Koda. Where are you going?"

"I'm going to ride around a little to see if I can spot him. People like that are never too far away. They like to see their victims scramble and be afraid. I would bet a million dollars he's watching."

"Why don't you come over here and assault me with your tongue like you promised and forget about his deranged ass."

Koda looked at me, sucked his teeth, and walked out the door.

"Damn it," I said, hitting my fist against my thigh. "I should have never told his ass." Fuck you, Jhovan, for ruining my morning.

AFTER GETTING DRESSED, I hopped in my brand-new Range Rover, courtesy of Koda, and made my way to the police station.

As I pulled into the parking lot, I noticed Koda was already there. He hopped out of his car, trekked over, and opened my door.

"I didn't know if you were coming or not. You didn't seem worried enough for me. I wanted to make sure you came and did what you needed to do," he said. "I've been waiting on you."

"Koda, you and I don't lie to each other. If I say I'm going to do something, then I'm going to do it, but I think it's super sweet the way you care about me. I know you mean well."

"I really do, Zaya. I don't know what I would do if his ignorant ass did something to you. I'd set this whole city on fire. Me, your mama, and your stepfather would set it off in this bitch," we both cackled.

"Now come on and get in here to handle this business so you can get to work. I promise I will make up for this morning. As soon as the kids go to bed...your ass is mine."

"No, my ass is mine. The pussy, however, is all yours," I chuckled.

"I'll take it," he mumbled as he ushered me into the police station. After the report was filed, we kissed and went our separate ways.

CHAPTER 18

Oh, By The Way

I arrived at work to an empty parking lot which was ok with me. I was able to focus a lot better when I wasn't being disrupted. Before I stepped foot out my SUV, I drove around the back of the building and the sides to make sure Jhovan wasn't hiding out anywhere. Then I parked directly in the front. Cocking my gun first, I slid out my SUV and strolled into the office.

I set my bag on the desk and took a deep breath, letting the silence wrap around me. I was halfway through booting up my computer when I heard the faint jingle of keys and the squeal of the front door opening. My heart jumped, my hand instinctively brushing against the handle of my gun.

"Zaya?"

The familiar voice made me exhale. "Sylvia? You scared the shit outta me."

Her laughter filled the space, light and nostalgic. "Girl, I told you I'd be in early today. You just beat me to it."

I smiled, tension easing from my shoulders as I watched her walk in, iced latte in her hand, her curls bouncing the same way they did years ago. For a moment, it felt like nothing had changed. We were just two women trying to make it through another day.

She set her purse and sweater down and gave me a warm look. "You remember when we used to be the first ones here every morning? We'd sit in your office, drink that nasty vending machine coffee, and talk about life like we had all our shit together."

I chuckled, shaking my head. "Yeah, we really thought we knew something back then."

"Back then," she repeated softly, leaning against the counter. "Seems like a lifetime ago."

Silence stretched for a moment, heavier now. I could feel her studying me, her eyes full of something, guilt maybe. Then she sighed. "Zaya, there's something I've been meaning to tell you for a long time."

I frowned, "What's that?"

She hesitated, rubbing her hands together like she was searching for the right words. "I owe you an apology. For... for pushing you to go out with Jhovan all those years ago."

I blinked, unsure how to respond. "Girl, what are you talking about. It's not like you made me."

"I did though," she said quietly. "I really did. You didn't even want to go out with him, but I kept insisting. I thought I was doing something good. He'd just gotten out of the hospital, and I felt sorry for him."

The air shifted, cold and uneasy. "Hospital? For fucking what?" I asked slowly.

She nodded, eyes facing the floor. "Yeah, Mental hospital. He was in and out for years before that. They said he was bipolar at first, then later they said it was schizophrenia or maybe a mix of both. He had these...episodes. He wouldn't sleep for days, then crash for weeks. Sometimes he'd talk to people who weren't there, or think folks were following him."

I took a step back, my throat suddenly dry. "Wait- what? Sylvia, are you serious right now?"

Her eyes welled with tears. "I swear to you, I thought he was better. Kevin said the doctors said he was doing good, that he was stable. He looked like he was turning his life around and I just thought...maybe if he had someone like you, someone grounded and kind, it would keep him steady."

I stared at her, my mind spinning. "You mean to tell me you introduced me to a man fresh out the muthafuckin mental hospital and never thought to say a word to me about it?"

Tears slid down her face as she whispered, "I thought he was safe, Zaya. I thought love could fix him."

I felt the room tilt slightly. Everything I'd been through with Jhovan...the lies, the control, the anger simmering under the calm suddenly took on a different shape. I gripped the edge of the desk, trying to steady myself.

"Oh my God..." I breathed. Sylvia, you should've told me."

Her voice trembled. "I swear, Zaya...if I could take it back, I would. I thought I was helping him and maybe helping you find someone good too. I didn't know how broken he still was."

I couldn't speak for a moment. My heart was thundering in my chest, but not out of anger...out of realization. Pieces of the puzzle that never made sense started sliding into place. His temper, the way his moods flipped like a switch, the long stretches where he'd shut down completely and shut me out.

I pressed a hand to my mouth. "This...This makes so much sense. It explains a lot," I muttered. My God, Sylvia, I thought it was me. For the longest, I thought I was the problem."

She reached for me, her voice soft. "You were never the

problem, girl. You were just caught in the middle of something you didn't see coming."

I sank into my chair, staring blankly at the monitor that had gone dark again. My reflection looked different, older, wearier. "He used to stare off into space for hours," I whispered to myself. "Sometimes I'd ask what he was thinking, and he'd say, "They're talking to loud. I thought his ass was talking about the kids or the neighbors, but..."

I trailed off, stomach in knots.

Sylvia's face broke, "Zaya..."

Tears stung the corners of my eyes. "My babies, Sylvia. My babies...I let that man tuck them in, drive us places, talk to them, discipline them." My voice cracked as the words came out. "What if...what if he passed something down to them?"

She moved closer, crouching beside me. "Hey, don't do that. Don't start blaming yourself, and don't assume the worst. Your babies are smart and strong. You've given them love and stability. That's what matters most."

I shook my head, the tears spilling freely now. "But what if that's not enough? What if it's already in them, hiding somewhere? I've seen flashes of his anger in Jr. before. I thought it was just him being a brat but what if it's not?"

Sylvia reached up and took my hand. "You listen to me," she said firmly, her tone gentle but grounded. "You can't change what's in their blood, but you can shape what's in their hearts. You're breaking the cycle, Zaya. You already are."

I wiped my cheeks, breathing slowly until the trembling eased.

"I wish you'd told me sooner," I whispered, "but I know you meant well."

She nodded, tears sliding down her own face. "I did. I really did."

We sat there in silence for a while, the air thick with unspoken memories and regret.

Finally, I spoke again. "I just need to make sure my kids are safe. Not just from him, but from whatever pieces of him might still live in them. I have to know they'll be okay."

Sylvia squeezed my hand. "Then start there. Protect your peace and protect theirs. You can't change Jhovan's past, but you can change what happens next."

I nodded slowly, my mind already racing with a fierce determination to cover not only their bodies but their minds as well.

By the time Friday rolled around, I'd replayed that conversation with Sylvia so many times, I started hearing it in my dreams. So, I did what any woman with a crisis did??? I called my mama.

"Baby, pack a bag and get here," she said before I could

even finish explaining. "Sounds like you need your mama and a hot meal."

That's how I knew it was serious, when she offered both.

By Saturday morning, the house smelled like smothered pork chops, collard greens, and all the things that make you forget your problems. At least until the dishes are done. Mama was already bossing Koda around like he was one of her own kids, and to my surprise, he didn't seem to mind.

"Boy, don't just stand there lookin' good, gone stir that pot before it burns!" she barked, waving her spoon like a weapon.

Koda grinned, dutifully stirring. "Yes, ma'am. I got it. Don't want no trouble with you."

"Smart man," she said with a nod, satisfied. "Zaya always picks the hard-headed ones, so it's nice to see a little common sense in the house for once."

I nearly choked on my tea. "Mama!"

"What? I'm just saying! Ain't that what the kids say now a days. 'I'm just sayin,' or something like that."

When we finally sat down to eat, the laughter died down, and I knew I couldn't keep it in any longer. "Mama, Sylvia told me something this week. Something about Jhovan."

That got her attention real quick. Fork down. Eyebrows raised. "Oh, Lord. What that fool done now?"

I hesitated, then took a deep breath. "She said he used to be in a mental hospital. Bipolar. Schizophrenia. She thought he was rehabilitated."

Mama blinked. Then blinked again. "Well, that explains everything."

Koda's head popped up. "Everything?"

"Chile, yes," Mama said, waving her fork. "That man been off since the first day I met him. You remember when he came to Thanksgiving talking about how the turkey was watchin' him? I said, 'No baby, that's the gravy boat reflection, now pass the rolls.'"

Koda burst out laughing, nearly spitting his drink across the table.

"Mama!" I groaned, though I couldn't help the smile tugging at my lips.

"What? You know I'm right! I told you then he wasn't wrapped tight. You said he was 'deep.' I said, no baby, that's a hole in his logic."

Even I had to laugh at that. "You always say you liked him at first."

"I lied," she said bluntly. "I liked his mama's pound cake. That's it."

Koda leaned back in his chair, still grinning. "So now what you gonna do, baby?"

I sighed, "I don't know. I just want to make sure the kids are okay. I keep thinking...what if they inherited something?"

Mama reached across the table and patted my hand. "Then we deal with it. You hear me? We pray, we watch, we love 'em through it. Ain't no curse bigger than what God can fix."

Koda nodded. "And you're not alone, Zaya. You got me now. Whatever comes, we'll face it together."

Mama side-eyed him with a smirk. "Mmm-hmm. That's cute. Just remember that when she wakes up at 3 a.m. overthinking and you gotta talk her down with pancakes."

He laughed. "Deal. I make a mean pancake."

"Good," Mama said, leaning back smugly. "Welcome to the family, baby. Now pass me that hot sauce before I lose my religion."

The laughter returned, softening the edges of the truth that had been weighing me down. I felt lighter. Still scared, still uncertain but surrounded by love, and that made all the difference.

After dinner, the house smelled like cornbread and laughter. Koda was in the kitchen washing dishes or pretending to, because I could still hear the water running but no clanking. Mama was sprawled across the couch, half-asleep with her plate still in her lap. Samson was still at work, pulling a double yet again and the kids were out on the deck in the backyard catching fireflies.

I leaned against the doorway and just watched them for a minute. Koda humming off-key to some old blues song, Mama softly snoring like she'd just preached a whole sermon and left it all on the pulpit.

I thought about Sylvia's words again, the hospital, the diagnosis, and the guilt in her voice. It all still hurt, but it didn't own me anymore. The truth had stopped being a knife and started being a bandage.

I looked at my kids' pictures on the wall. All three of them, smiling wide with ice cream all over their faces. I smiled to myself. Whatever they might've inherited from their father, they also had me. They had love, structure, faith, and a mama who wasn't afraid to fight for their peace.

Koda poked his head out of the kitchen. "You gonna just stand there looking fine, or you wanna help dry these dishes?"

I laughed softly. "You were doing such a good job faking it, I didn't wanna interrupt."

He grinned and tossed the towel over his shoulder. "I can stop pretending real quick if you wanna join me."

From the couch, Mama mumbled without opening her eyes, "Y'all better not start no mess in my kitchen. I got one good eye open."

We both laughed, quiet enough not to wake her completely.

I walked over, took the towel from Koda, and brushed my shoulder against his. "Thank you," I whispered.

He looked down at me, serious for a moment. "For what?"

"For being here. For not running from all this."

He shook his head, a small smile forming. "I told you before, I don't scare easy. Besides, I like the way you fight your battles. Even when you're tired, you still show up."

My throat tightened, but in a good way this time.

As he went back to the sink, I glanced once more at Mama snoring softly, Koda humming, and the glow of the lamp filling the room. The world outside might've been chaotic, uncertain and full of unanswered questions but in this moment, I had everything I needed.

Real, quiet, healing peace.

And for now, that was enough.

CHAPTER 19

The Message

J ust as I started to turn off the kitchen light, my phone buzzed across the counter...one new message.

From an unknown number.

> Unknown number: We need to talk. It's about Jhovan.

I froze, the warmth in my chest fading into a chill.

Dammit, every time I exhale, something else happens. I'm getting sick of this shit.

The text glowed against the dark screen, the words pulsing like a heartbeat.

> Unknown number: We need to talk. It's about Jhovan.

I stared at it for a long moment, trying to decide if I should answer or throw it in the backyard for the armadillos to play with. My pulse thudded in my ears, slow at first, then faster, until I could practically feel it echoing in my throat.

Koda's voice drifted from behind me. "You okay, Zaya?"

I turned slightly, forcing a smile that fooled neither of us. "Yeah... just work stuff."

He frowned. "At nine o'clock at night?"

"Mmhmm." I shoved the phone into my back pocket like it had betrayed me. "You know how it is. People always got questions they could've asked before the weekend."

Koda tilted his head, studying me with those sharp eyes that didn't miss a thing. "You do realize I'm damn near a human lie detector, right? You sure that's all it is?"

I nodded too quickly. "Positive."

"Alright." He kissed my forehead, lingering just long enough for my heartbeat to calm. "I'm about to take your mama her blanket. She snoring so loud she probably gonna wake the neighbors."

That made me smile, even if just for a second. "Good luck with that."

As soon as he disappeared into the living room, I pulled my phone back out. My fingers hovered over the screen.

> Me: Who is this?

The reply came fast.

> Unknown number : It's Sylvia. Please don't be mad. But he's been reaching out to me.

My stomach dropped.

> Me: Jhovan?

> Unknown Number: Yes. He called from a blocked number three times today. Said he just wanted to "make things right."

> Me; Make things right" with who? With me? The kids? Did you answer him?

> Unknown number: No. But he left a voicemail. You should hear it.

> Me: Sylvia… send it.

It came through a few seconds later — one minute long.

I stared at the screen, thumb hovering over the play button, afraid to hear the voice I'd worked so hard to erase from my life.

Then I hit play.

My stomach began to churn the minute my name rolled off his lips.

"Zaya, you, me and the kids will be taking that ride soon."

The phone nearly slipped from my hand. That voice... calm, smooth, and chillingly familiar crawled down my spine like a piece of ice.

"Taking that ride soon."

I replayed it just to make sure I hadn't imagined it, but the words hit the same every time. I started to feel nauseous and then I remembered what I had to do.

For a few seconds, the only sound in the kitchen was the refrigerator and my uneven breathing.

"Zaya?"

Koda's voice snapped me back to the present. I quickly locked the screen and set the phone face down on the counter, trying to pull my face into something close to normal.

He stepped closer, the concern already written all over his face. "You look... vexed. What's going on?"

"Nothing," I started, but my voice betrayed me, trembling just enough for him to catch it.

"Zaya." His tone softened. "Talk to me."

I took a deep breath, the words tumbling out before I

could stop them. "He called Sylvia. Three times. He left a voicemail."

Koda went still, his jaw tightening. "What'd he say?"

I swallowed hard. "He said... me and the kids will be taking that ride soon. He didn't even sound like himself. He sounded like a completely different person."

For a moment, neither of us spoke. The air felt heavy, disturbed.

Koda's calm dropped, replaced with something else. "That man don't give a shit about that restraining order or anything else. I'm going to have to stop him myself."

I shook my head, panic rising. "Koda, no. Don't go looking for him, it's just gonna stir him up. Let me think."

He looked at me like I'd lost my mind. "Stir him up? Zaya, Stirred isn't a good enough word to describe his ass. That was a warning, Zaya. That's not a social call!"

Before I could respond, Mama's voice carried from the living room. "What y'all whisperin' 'bout in there? You know I can hear stress, right?"

Koda and I shared a look.

"Mama, it's fine," I yelled, forcing calmness I didn't feel. "Go back to sleep."

"I'm awake now," she announced, appearing in the doorway with her scarf halfway off her head and her house shoes on the wrong feet. "And unless you whisperin' about Jesus, I suggest you say it loud enough for me to hear it."

Koda tried, bless him. "It's just... uh, work stuff, Miss Ann."

Mama squinted at him. "Boy, don't lie in my face. You too fine for that. What's going on?"

I sighed. "Jhovan called Sylvia."

That got her attention. "From where? The depths of hell?"

Koda tried not to laugh but failed miserably.

"Mama!" I groaned.

She crossed her arms. "Don't 'Mama' me. I knew he was trouble the moment he said he didn't eat leftovers. That's the mark of a disturbed man right there."

Koda snorted, turning his head to hide it.

I shook my head but couldn't help a small laugh through my nerves. "Mama, this is serious."

"I *am* serious. Only a crazy man thinks food expires after one night in the fridge." She walked over, lowered her voice. "What he want, baby?"

I told her, and for once, she didn't have a comeback. Just a slow, steady look that said she was already running through a plan.

Finally, she said, "Alright then. The kids are already asleep in their bedroom, Zaya, you sleep in the guest room and Koda, you take that couch by the window. If that fool even breathes in this direction, he gon' meet Jesus quicker than he planned."

Koda smiled faintly. "Yes, ma'am. I'll be right there."

"You've got your gun don't you Mr. Officer Man?" she questioned.

"Of course. I don't move without it," he responded.

Mama nodded, satisfied, and shuffled back toward her room. "Now, both of y'all cut that whisperin' out. I need my beauty rest in case I gotta go to jail tomorrow."

When she disappeared, I exhaled a laugh that turned into a sigh. Koda slipped an arm around my waist, pulling me gently against him.

"We're not gonna let him near you," he murmured. "Or the kids. You hear me?"

I nodded, leaning into his warmth. "I hear you."

But even as I said it, my eyes flicked toward the dark window and for a split second, I could've sworn I saw movement outside.

CHAPTER 20

A New Dawn

The sun had barely risen when I awoke, my body aching from a night of tossing, turning, and jumping at every little sound. I rubbed my eyes and glanced around the room. The house was quiet, but the heaviness from the previous night still clung to me like a wet t-shirt. I went into the kids' room to get a quick look at them. They were sound asleep, gently purring like three little bears. I closed the door and sauntered to the kitchen to find Mama moving around like a one-woman army. Pancakes flipping, bacon sizzling, and coffee brewing.

Koda had stayed on the couch by the window, snoring softly, but I could tell he'd been awake half the night, listening too.

Mama, yelled from the kitchen, "Come get these plates for the babies and tell them to eat it out back on the deck.

Us three have got some planning to do and they don't need to know what we're plotting."

I did what I was told and returned to the kitchen.

"You two better sit down before I decide y'all need lessons in manners," she barked, sliding a plate of pancakes toward me. "You look like a ghost that just saw somebody he didn't know was dead."

Koda smirked, grabbing a plate. "Ghost? I'd say zombie, more like. Crazy hair, tired eyes... she's walking the fine line between cute and terrifying."

Mama shot him a look, "You need to clarify what you mean Mr. Officer man because bedhead and all...my Baby-girl is gorgeous."

"You're right," Koda said, holding up his hands in mock surrender, "I'd let her haunt me any day."

I groaned but couldn't stop the laugh escaping my lips.

Mama snorted. "Y'all ridiculous. Ghost or not, we gotta focus. What we need is a plan. And maybe a baseball bat. Preferably both."

Koda laughed. "I like that idea. Baseball bat first, plan second."

Mama shot him a death glare. "You better not be joking, boy. This ain't the time for humor."

Koda grinned anyway. "Mama, you know I never joke about safety. I wasn't joking about the baseball bat *and* the plan. I was thinking add a couple of guns to the mix."

I shook my head, sipping my coffee. "You two are ridiculous. But seriously... what do we do?"

Mama leaned closer, lowering her voice dramatically, like we were plotting a heist. "First, we make sure the kids are never alone. Second, we find out exactly what Sylvia knows. And third..." She leaned back, pointing a pancake-flipping spatula at me. "We make sure that man knows he picked the wrong mama and the wrong woman. And that nobody touches your babies while I'm alive."

Koda nodded, trying not to grin too widely. "Got it. Step three sounds like my favorite."

Mama shot him another look, muttering, "I swear, he's worse than your step-father sometimes."

I laughed, shaking my head.

Koda, added, "Step four: make sure we watch all surroundings. Even when you don't think you saw anything...look again."

"Step four is the smart one," Mama said approvingly, then paused. "Step five: Yall get in there and wash those dishes."

We cackled, feeling some of the weight from last night lift. Yeah, Jhovan was still a threat, unpredictable and dangerous. But I had my mama, my kids, and Koda. And together, we'd be ready for whatever came next.

Even if it meant fighting a grown man while armed with pancakes and sass.

Monday came too fast, and I couldn't shake the lingering fear. I needed to make sure my children were safe at all times. Koda and I left them with Mama and Samson and drove to the school to officially withdraw them. They would spend the rest of the year being homeschooled. I couldn't take any chances. My hands gripped the steering wheel tightly, eyes flicking constantly to the rearview mirror. Scanning for anything unusual.

"Baby, you've got to relax. You're going to rip the steering wheel out of its column." Koda, muttered.

He was right, I needed to calm down but knowing what I knew about Jhovan's history wouldn't allow it. Once I left the school and the paperwork was done, I felt a little lighter, though the knots in my shoulders still remained.

Koda stayed in the car while I took care of business. Waiting patiently like always. Next, I was off to my job to advise India of the immediate need of a leave of absence to get my affairs in order. Or at least until I could get this thing with my ex-husband under control. I didn't want to put anyone else in danger by having him show up unexpectedly again and scaring the Bejesus out of all of us.

I pulled into the office parking lot. My stomach sank when I realized no one else was there. The silence was oppressive, and the empty lobby made my nerves twist a little tighter but as always, Koda assured me everything would be ok. I kissed him and told him I'd be back shortly. He insisted on waiting outside in the car to watch the perimeter. I trekked into the office and sat at my desk, fidgeting while waiting for India to arrive.

It wasn't long before Sylvia appeared, striding in with that same energy. Calm but sharp.

"Good morning," she said, sliding into the chair across from me. "You look like you haven't slept in days."

"You don't know the half of it," I muttered. "After you sent those text messages, I couldn't. Hell, I couldn't even rest. That shit stayed on my mind my entire weekend. Not only my mind...my mama's mind and my man's mind too."

"I'm sorry to have interrupted your weekend but you had to know. I didn't want to keep anything else from you. Shit, if a pen drops and leaves a mark on your carpet...I'm telling," we cackled.

"You don't have to apologize. I appreciate you for looking out."

"Zaya, that's the least I could do." Sylvia's face paled slightly. "He wouldn't leave me alone. Every time I thought it stopped, another message or another call came through. I had to call the phone company and change my number."

"I get it, Sylvia. I had to do the same thing."

We shared a tense laugh, the absurdity of the situation

briefly easing the weight on our shoulders. It was a small moment of solidarity, but it helped.

"I see that fine ass bodyguard is sitting in your car. Is he going to stay out there the whole time you're at work?"

"First, he's my man not my bodyguard and no. I'm here to tell India I must take a leave of absence for a while. Hopefully, she will understand and not give my job away. I had to take drastic measures when it came to my children's safety and because of it... I have to be home with them." I sighed. "This shit with Jhovan has really been life altering in a major way. Moving, new house, new car, watching my back every second of the day. I mean, Sylvia. This shit is exhausting."

"I really do hate this for you. Hopefully he will find someone else soon and move on to terrorizing them instead of you," she laughed.

"He has two girlfriends. I don't see why he won't leave me alone. I gave him to their asses. Guess they didn't know what they had after all. A batshit crazy narcissist with bipolar and schizophrenia."

Just as we were starting to get comfortable, talking quietly, sharing theories and venting our frustrations... movement in the far corner of the office stopped me dead in my tracks.

I froze. My pulse shot into overdrive.

Before I could react, Jhovan was charging at me full-speed. He came out of nowhere...silent and powerful. It was as if a shadow came to life. My scream caught in my throat as he lunged, hands wrapping around my arms and slamming me into the wall. Pain exploded along my side as I tried to kick free. My heart hammered in my ears.

"Zaya!" Sylvia's voice sliced through the panic.

I barely had time to register her presence before I heard the shot. It rang out like a cannon. Then dead silence.

Jhovan staggered back, but not for long. His hands clawed at me again, his grip was iron strong, eyes wide and wild.

"Get off me!" I screamed. Kicking and twisting, He grabbed my neck, pushing upwards, sweeping me off my feet.

Sylvia fired again. Slowing his assault, but he was like the fuckin' return of the living dead. I could feel the pulse of his rage against me. It was almost inhuman. Gurgling, he fought through pain and fury. I was terrified as I felt myself slipping in and out of consciousness.

"Zaya! Duck!" Sylvia shouted but I couldn't. I couldn't do anything. I couldn't move. Couldn't breathe. Sylvia cracked him across the back of the head with the butt of her gun but it didn't phase him. With a firm grip still around my neck with one hand, Jhovan swung back at her with the other.

The next few seconds were a blur... me scrambling,

fighting for air, and attempting to pry his hands from my neck. It felt like my eyes were bulging out my head. For a moment, Jhovan stumbled, grabbing his chest, swaying from the pain. I could only pray the bullets that had entered his body was doing their job and stopping the monster I previously called my husband. Finally he let go and stumbled back. Before I could fully take a deep breath and fall to the ground, his hands found my neck again.

I tried to fight but I had nothing left. Nothing but flashes. Flashes of my children's faces as they waved goodbye to me in the mornings. Flashes of my mother sitting on her couch watching Tv while sipping her chamomile tea. And last but not least, flashes of Koda's crooked smile gleaming at me as he gently stroked my cheek. I weakly opened my eyes just as I started to fade, and saw Koda running through the door. ....then nothing.

The line between life and death is minuscule and I knew I'd crossed over. That was until I heard the last shot rang out. It was as if it brought me back to life. I couldn't open my eyes but I could faintly hear the gurgling just as I'd seen in my vision. I felt myself fall to the floor.

I could vaguely feel Koda shaking me, pleading with me, praying over me, and before he could lay me back to administer CPR, I came to.

I opened my eyes to see Jhovan collapsed on the floor and was clawing at the carpet. His body twisted in pain.

Blood blossomed across his chest just as I noticed his blood was splattered across mine.

"Koda yanked me out of Jhovan's reach as he tried one last violent lunge.

With Koda's help. I stood and stepped back, lungs and throat still on fire and heart hammering. Koda, grabbed me and held me so tight, I thought he would snap me in two.

Sylvia had saved my life and for that, Koda grabbed her and hugged her as well.

When the paramedics arrived, he was still alive, still thrashing weakly. They loaded him into the ambulance, sirens wailing and I felt a small relief. Secretly, I wished it was the coroners picking him up instead.

Pamela popped in at the last minute. She'd heard of a shooting at an interior decorators' firm from her police scanner and raced to the scene. She pulled up, sirens blaring and forgot to put the car in park. Running into the building, she ran straight towards me, snatched me up and hugged me like a mother hugs her child.

"Don't you ever in your muthafuckin life scare me like that again. Girl, I thought that crazy ass man had taken my best friend from me. Look at my face bitch. I've been ugly crying the whole way here. I looked in the mirror and saw a damn banshee only to realize it was me," she gently chuckled through the tears. She grabbed my face and pushed it to the side. "Oh my God, Zaya. Your fucking neck. That bastard really tried to kill you. I hope they beat the shit out of him in the back of that damn car."

"Yes he did but nawl, bestie. I'm still here. Thanks to Sylvia. She took his ass down. That was the scariest shit I've ever experienced. I'm going to definitely need therapy after this."

"Listen, I did what I had to do. Zaya and I went together to buy our first gun. After that, we practically lived at the range. That shit paid off didn't it girl," Sylvia said proudly.

"It sure did, Sylvia. I thought you would never get a good shot."

"The shot wasn't the problem. Every time you moved your head, he moved his big ass head too. I didn't want to shoot the wrong person. I was scared the bullet would go through him into you," she admitted.

Standing by my side, Koda said, "Well I'm just glad this all worked out. I was sitting in the car with the music up, clueless as hell. The only reason I came in was to see what was taking so long. I couldn't believe my eyes, seeing that big ass monster attacking my baby. My first instinct as an officer was to neutralize the threat. I wanted to shoot until his ass wasn't moving but just like Sylvia, I didn't want to harm my baby."

Just as we were recapping our feelings, a police sergeant

named Sergeant Brooks walked towards us. He advised if Jhovan survived, he'd arranged for him to be returned to the mental hospital because of his history and he'd be under heavy supervision. He would no longer be a threat to anyone but the pads in his room.

Sylvia put a hand on my shoulder. "Whether he lives or dies isn't important right now. You're alive and he can't bother you again. That's what matters the most. And Mr. Sergeant Officer man, please keep his ass locked away. I mean even when you think he's good, just know he isn't. That mental hospital is where he belongs."

"I will do my best," Sergeant Brooks whispered before turning around and handling his crime scene. He winked at Sylvia and we all cackled.

LATER, we learned he did survive and a cold, hard, chill covered my body.

For now, the storm had passed. The house was quiet. My kids were back in school and safe. And maybe, just maybe, I could finally let go of the tension that had a stronghold on my life for months.

The first time I exhaled in days felt like I'd been holding my breath underwater, gasping for air, and finally breaking the surface.

I LEANED back in my office chair, tipping it slightly, letting my feet swing. The quiet of the office was refreshing. No calls, no footsteps lurking in the shadows, no blood-stained memories from last week haunting my mind. Just quiet. Just... me.

I chuckled softly. *"Who even am I without this constant panic?"* I muttered, sipping my coffee.

It felt like a crime. Almost a sin... the freedom to be mundane, to laugh at nothing, to stretch my arms above my head and not feel a muscle paralyze with fear.

I walked over to the window, letting the morning sun warm my face. Outside, cars passed, people walked dogs, and life carried on as if nothing had happened. And for a moment, it was like I was watching a movie, not living it.

I spun back around to my desk and caught sight of the kids' artwork taped to the bulletin board. Crayon rainbows, stick-figure families, scribbled hearts. My chest swelled. That was why I fought. That was why I survived.

A knock at the door made me jump, and I swung it open to find Mama, arms crossed and smirk in place.

"Well, look at you. Sitting there like you own the place," she said, voice dripping with humor. "You got that 'I survived a horror movie' glow."

I laughed, letting it spill out. "Let me tell it, I did survive one."

Mama shook her head, stepping in and leaning against the desk. "You did, baby. You did. And now? You get to enjoy the peace."

I twirled around in my chair. "Enjoy the peace..." I repeated, savoring the words. "I forgot what that felt like."

"You better not get too carried away," she warned. "Life likes to sneak up on you when you start feeling carefree."

I shrugged, grinning. "Then I'll enjoy it while it lasts. Coffee in hand, sunshine on my face, no psycho lurking in the office. That's my plan."

Mama laughed. "Mmm-hmm. I like it. Just don't forget, you've got people watching your back. Koda, me, even Sylvia. You don't have to do it all alone, baby."

I smiled warmly, the carefree feeling settling deep in my chest. I allowed myself to relax, to laugh, to imagine a life beyond fear.

I spun my chair once more, just for the fun of it and let my laughter echo in the quiet office.

The storm was gone. Life felt soft again. Simple, safe, and gloriously full of love.

The End

Epilogue

The laughter of children filled the air. Jr, Trinity and Thalia tumbled across the rug, chasing one another, squealing in delight, their energy infectious. Koda leaned back in his chair, arms crossed, watching them with that same crooked smile that had carried me through the darkest days.

I laughed softly, shaking my head as I stirred my coffee. "They never stop asking about their father," I muttered.

"Yeah," Koda said, glancing at me knowingly. "Have you made a decision yet?"

I hesitated. "Yes, but the kids' wide, curious eyes and endless questions finally wore me down. I broke and told them yes. But... we do it carefully. Mama's going with us."

The trip to the mental hospital was a blur of cautious

steps and tense anticipation. The kids clutched my hands tightly, excitement and fear mingled in their expressions.

And then we saw him. Jhovan.

Nothing could have prepared us for the sheer intensity of his presence. He screamed as he called my name over and over. He spit, thrashed and called me every obscenity known to man. The chaotic energy that had haunted my life for so long was now spilling over in full force. Sheer horror covered my babies' faces as their little hands gripped mine tighter than ever.

I knew, immediately, that this would be the last time. No child should witness that kind of terror. "Let's get out of here. I knew this was a bad idea," I said firmly. "Never again." And with Mama guiding us out, I made sure we never returned.

Two years later, news came that one of the bullets from the attack shifted inside Jhovan's body, causing his death. I felt a strange mix of relief and sorrow, but mostly relief. The threat that had hung over our lives was gone.

Koda, ever the dutiful son, traveled to Tallahassee to bring his father closer to him for his final days. Surrounded by Koda, me, the kids, Koda's sister, and her four children, his father passed peacefully in his sleep.

We kept our promise to Koda's father to do things the proper way. Weeks later, we married on a warm spring day, our children laughing at our vows and stealing kisses from our cheeks. Soon after, we soon welcomed a set of twin boys into our family, double the chaos, double the love. The house was always filled with laughter, warmth, and music, a sanctuary full with nothing but love.

I launched my own interior design firm, building a team that reflected my vision and heart. And when I offered Sylvia the role of C.O.O, she accepted with that sly grin I remembered from our younger days.

Life was full of second chances, laughter, and love and we were finally living it.

Koda slid an arm around me, pulling me close. "You happy?" he asked quietly.

I rested my head against his shoulder, feeling the warmth of the family we'd built. "Happiest I've ever been," I whispered.

And I meant it.

The house was alive, the kids were safe, the past was behind us, and the future stretched out bright and wide.

Sylvia's Blind Date

One Friday evening, after a particularly successful project, I set Sylvia up on a blind date with one of Koda's officer buddies.

"You're trying to get me hooked up with one of his friends," she accused, arms crossed and a smirk tugging at her lips.

"Maybe," I said innocently. "Or maybe I just know he's perfect for you."

She laughed, shaking her head. "You're impossible."

"Yes, some would say that. I teased.

As she got ready to leave, I watched her with a fond smile.

Saturday night arrived, and Sylvia was a vision to see... curls bouncing, skin tight dress, sexy red lipstick, and heels clicking as she strutted into the restaurant.

I sat in the corner booth with Koda, pretending not to watch, but I absolutely was. He leaned over, chuckling. "You know she's gonna interrogate that poor man, right?"

"That's the point," I whispered, eyes gleaming. "Better she find out now if he's got any... hidden issues."

Koda smirked. "Like a metal detector for crazy?"

"Exactly," I said. "Only hers is set to maximum sensitivity."

Across the room, Sylvia's date, Officer Alexander Brooks, stood as she approached. Tall, handsome, charming smile. He extended a hand. "Ms. Sylvia, pleasure to officially meet you."

"Oh, we'll see," she said with a teasing smile, shaking it firmly. "Pleasure's earned, not given."

Koda choked back a laugh. "She's starting already."

We ordered appetizers and pretended to mind our business while Sylvia launched into her famous *interview mode.*

"So, Officer Brooks," she began, sitting upright like a lawyer at deposition. "You ever been arrested? Suspended? Fired? Divorced? Engaged to anyone currently or previously incarcerated?"

He blinked, taken aback. "Uh, no ma'am. None of the above."

"Good," she said, scribbling on her napkin with the pen she pulled from her purse. "Mental health history?"

He froze, fork halfway to his mouth. "Excuse me?"

"Mental health," she repeated smoothly. "You ever been diagnosed with bipolar disorder? Schizophrenia? Narcissism? Split personalities? Anything that would require... say... medication or a padded room?"

I nearly spit out my drink. Koda leaned in, whispering, "She's out here doing background checks in real time."

Poor Alex blinked, his smile faltering but polite. "No, ma'am. Just regular stress like any cop, but I handle it with prayer, protein shakes, and therapy once a month."

Sylvia nodded approvingly. "Therapy? Oh, that's good. Healthy coping. Okay, next question... you ever stalked anybody?"

"*Sylvia!*" I hissed from across the room, pretending to wave like I wasn't dying of laughter.

She waved me off. "It's a legitimate question!"

Alex laughed nervously. "Uh... no. Can't say I have."

"Alright," she said, leaning back, arms crossed. "We're making progress."

He looked at her, amused. "Do I get to ask you any questions, or is this a one-way interview?"

Sylvia smiled sweetly. "You can try but I'm perfect on paper. And if you do find something, it's probably a scheme set up by a hater."

He laughed so hard, he grabbed his side and something in his eyes softened. "Okay, I like you," he said honestly. "You're intense, but I like it."

She blinked, caught off guard for half a second before that sly grin returned. "Good... Maybe we'll get dessert after all."

From our booth, I clasped my hands over my mouth, trying not to squeal. "Oh my God, he passed!"

Koda chuckled, wrapping an arm around me. "That man deserves a medal. She's not easy to impress."

"I think she met her match," I whispered.

Across the room, Sylvia laughed at something Alex

said, tossing her hair over her shoulder, her guard lowering just enough for genuine joy to slip through.

It was perfect. Full circle.

Everyone had found peace... messy, beautiful, earned peace.

Koda pressed a kiss to my temple. "Looks like you have a new talent. Go ahead matchmaker."

I smiled, heart full. "I'm not the only one who deserves a happy ending."

We clinked glasses, and I looked across the room one last time. Sylvia laughing, Alex smiling, the world finally righting itself.

L.L. Momon is a passionate storyteller who crafts emotionally rich, character-driven novels that explore healing, love, and resilience. Born and raised in Tuskegee, Alabama, and now residing in Florida, Momon brings Southern warmth and depth to every story she writes.

A nail technician by trade and an intuitive introvert at heart, she draws inspiration from the complexities of real-life relationships and personal growth. As a wife and mother and lover girl, she deeply values the strength of family, and that love radiates through the pages of her work.

With six published novels to her name, including her latest, *Loyalty Bound Me, Love Freed Me*, L.L. Momon is known for delivering raw, honest stories centered on strong, imperfect Black characters navigating trauma, passion, and redemption.

When she's not writing, you'll find her creating beauty with her hands, enjoying quiet moments with her family, cooking up soul-soothing meals, or binge-watching her favorite TV shows. Through every story, L.L. Momon reminds readers that even the most broken hearts are capable of healing and that love, when nurtured, is a force worth believing in.

instagram.com/authoressllmomon

facebook.com/authorllmomon

tiktok.com/authoressllmomon

amazon.com/author/llmomon

goodreads.com/authorllmomon

Also by L. L. Momon

Whittling Wood

Whittling Wood 2

A Savage and Her Wicked Ways

A Savage and His Lying Tongue

To Love the Broken & Unhealed

Loyalty Bound Me, Love Freed Me

The Author's Website authoressllmomon.square.site

https://linktr.ee/authoressllmomon

www.ingramcontent.com/pod-product-compliance
Lightning Source LLC
Chambersburg PA
CBHW050340030726
47503CB00008B/2533

* 9 7 9 8 9 9 4 8 9 9 4 2 7 *